DARK REVELATIONS

Vampire Matchmaking Agency

Book II

Dark Revelations:
Edited by: Jennifer Miller
Book Formatting: Jennifer Eaton
Cover Designer: DeliciousNightsDesigns.com

To everyone searching for a light in the darkness...

PROLOGUE

3 YEARS AGO...

"So, you ready to eat? Are we hunting tonight or just going out back for one of the feeders?" Leila Toussaint wanted more than anything to make the asshole pay for what he'd done to her progeny, but she wanted it to be Farrah's choice.

The target was a human male who'd outright rejected Farrah following a hookup on *sendmeamatch.com.* In truth, he didn't deserve to even be in Farrah's presence for anything other than feeding. There was something inherently wrong with humans getting the better of vampires.

Leila wasn't keen on mating, but Farrah Grant was not of the same mindset. She was delicate and kind. One who wanted what was best for the world and herself—whether they were vampire or other.

"Ugh, I hate the feeders. Their veins are always unstable," Farrah said. "There's nothing like feeding from an untapped vein. You know what I mean? I'd rather get a bag from the fridge and turn on the Hallmark Channel."

"Lame, but yeah, I do. So it sounds like we're hunting... How about we go see make-a-match dude?" Leila waited... the lights and sounds of Melody, her club in Harmony Park, downtown Detroit, filling the background like a mellowed-out Jeopardy tune.

"It's *sendmeamatch*."

"Whatevs. Matchmaker, matchmaker, send me whoever the hell, let's go over there."

Farrah's honey-brown eyes glossed over, her disdain evident. "No. And fucking no. He doesn't deserve the ecstasy of a bite."

In return, Leila fought hard to calm her domineering urges. She was working on being less of a bitch about Farrah's desire to find love. It wasn't Farrah's fault that Leila had allowed some angel to steal her heart with little more than a few pretty words a hundred years ago. "What you should have done was charmed that ass last night. Sure, he wouldn't have remembered a damn thing this morning, but at least you wouldn't have gotten dumped."

"I can't even with you. I thought we were going to date for a while. Isn't it wrong to feed off him with friends? I don't want the karma behind something like that."

"He left you sitting alone in a restaurant while he picked up some chick and left with her. Mind you, leaving you with the check."

"I know, but we weren't exactly hitting it off in person. I'm kind of glad it didn't go any further. I would have had to wipe his memory and all that. A few orgasms, *if* I was lucky, isn't worth that."

"You aren't sleeping with the right people, my friend.

C'mon... let's go. His veins are untapped... He'll be as fresh as a daisy or some other human bullcrap."

"Girl"—Farrah waved her hands in objection —"you're just thirsty as hell. I'm not going to show up at this dude's house. With a friend in tow. Random as fuck. Do you know what he'll think? No. I don't give a care if he won't remember it. It's too good for him."

"All right. So, we go in through the window on some old Bram Stoker shit?"

"No. Really, I'll pass on that." Following a moment of what appeared to be internal debate, Farrah rolled her eyes. "Yes, fine. We'll get over there. I'll knock on the door all like, *yes, I brought my friend by and we just want to talk to you for a second.* Okay?" The mocking tone in her voice emphasized exactly how much she hated the idea.

"Yes and yes."

"So, this is technically not hunting, though."

Despite Farrah's deliberation, Leila could barely contain her glee over the revenge mission. He deserved it, didn't he? "But it'll feel like it."

Farrah sucked her teeth. "C'mon. Let's go. He lives all the way downriver."

There was a hint of resistance remaining in Farrah's voice, but Leila pressed. "Driving or flying?"

"Driving. I have my Benz outside." Farrah smiled. She'd never been extremely fond of flying. In fact, in the last year, Leila could count the number of times she'd seen her fledgling take to air travel.

"I like that car."

"Yeah, me too. Pay the man. It's almost midnight. I'm fucking starving. I was so distraught, I didn't eat anything at sundown."

"Not even a snack? What is wrong with you? You

could have jumped one of these humans. Don't do that, sis. Do better."

"I don't need your judgment right now. Let's just go." Farrah laughed.

Leila pulled some folded cash from her bag and laid it on the counter. Since she was Farrah's maker, she was beholden to be her confidante and to make sure that Farrah had every necessity. A maker's responsibility was crazy, and until Farrah had her own recruit, Leila would see to it that Farrah was taken care of. Shit like getting her food if she couldn't hunt or protecting her from predators. And supporting all her progeny's silly ideas, like setting up a matchmaking agency for vampires. The latter was more likely than either of the others, thankfully.

And being her best friend.

They made it downriver to Monroe in just under forty minutes. It was a helluva drive. Had they flown, they could have cut that time by something like four hundred percent. Vampires *were* impatient, after all.

The lights were on in a typical ranch-style home as they sidled up to the curb. Farrah had said he was a real estate broker and that he had claimed to want the all-American dream, complete with a trophy wife and a riding lawnmower. It showed. Leila had dealt with humans like him before. While having nice things wasn't terrible, the thought that he was better than others for having them was a raggedy trait Leila couldn't overlook. Especially when he'd presupposed that Farrah wasn't worth his time based on his narrow, misogynistic viewpoint. Fuck that open vein—he was a loser.

Farrah got out of the car just as Leila reached the passenger side. They left it on the road instead of pulling into the driveway. It was dark in Monroe, a lot of it still good land for farming and raising a family—Michigan had lots of rural parts outside of Detroit. There were very few streetlights, making the location a popular vampire hunting ground. One Leila knew well.

"What a crappy, cookie-cutter house," she said. "You were legit going to date this douche?"

"Stop it. Nerds are awesome. And it's not crappy. It's just not the custom mansion or penthouse you're used to," Farrah replied, still defending him though he'd handed her heart back in a greasy brown paper bag. "It's got to be at least three thousand feet."

"Oh yeah, nerds are amazing. Except when they pres-elect females based on superficial shit, like a profile pic and bio. You could do better, but that's a story for another time. C'mon. Let's get this over with before you pass out from low blood sugar. Sheesh." Silently, Leila continued up the path. She glanced over her shoulder to find Farrah bringing up the rear.

"Yeah, I'm lightheaded now. Who's going to charm him?" Farrah whispered from a few steps behind.

"I can. I know you don't want this dude to remember you came by tonight. Stand by the garage."

Farrah nodded, following her directions. She leaned against the brick exterior in the corner of the shut garage door so he wouldn't see her cross in front of his windows. Once Farrah was in position, Leila strolled up the walkway and onto the low porch and rang the doorbell. Then she waited.

She heard his footsteps head across his faux marble floor in the foyer. "Who is it?" the d-bag called out.

"Um, my name is Leila. You don't know me, but I'm having a bit of car trouble. I think I could be out of gas, and I'm lost. Can I use your phone to call my friend? I forgot my charger too." Leila's voice was higher by no less than three octaves. Human men seemed to equate the probability of having sex with the pitch of a female's voice. Vampires had figured that shit out, and they'd been using it to their advantage ever since.

The door opened, and an abhorrent, rotund man disengaged the lock on the screen door. "I'm sorry, I didn't catch all that," he said. Spicy aftershave drifted off him as if he'd bathed in it, and she realized he must have had a date lined up because why on earth would someone do such a thing otherwise?

Fighting hard to stifle the impending eye roll, she continued. "I said... my name is Leila. I hope you can help me. I've run out of gas and my cell isn't charged." Her voice lowered. She was starting the charming process.

"Yeh, um... you need my help? Yes, you do. I can help you."

"I have a friend here. She's just over there. Can she come in too?"

Thirty seconds flat, and she had him under her spell and quite agreeable. In all sincerity, the guy wasn't exactly strong-willed and viable. He was just a catch for a human woman who was maybe heading to the other side of *prime*.

"Absolutely. I bet she's as pretty as you."

"Now, remember, you have no idea who she is..."

"None. None whatsoever."

"Okay." Leila paused for a moment before she called, "Farrah? Will you come now?"

Farrah didn't say anything. Instead, she quickly moved from her space in the shadows of the house to the front door.

"Hello, sir. What's your name?" Farrah asked him.

Being charmed was quite delicate for the first few minutes. They needed to be calm, gentle. The human brain always prepped itself before shutdown, as if on the edge of sleep, a loud noise or disturbance could bring them out of it... wake them up. They'd have to ensure those moments had passed before anything jarring or thought-provoking happened.

"Me? Oh, I'm Stan. This is my house. Can I invite you absolutely stunning ladies in?"

"Thank you, Stan. That is very gracious of you," Farrah said.

He moved aside to allow them entry, and they walked into the house. He had overdone the track lighting from the eighties, and everything in the joint was white or neutral tones. Someone must have told him it was trashy to have too much color in one place. Instead, the effect was sterile.

Farrah walked through and headed for the dining room, taking a seat at the table and propping her feet on top of it.

"Why don't you show me around, Stan," Leila prompted him. She glared at Farrah for not participating, but it was Leila's ruse, after all.

"Okay, I will."

They moved throughout the house as Stan explained every piece of furniture and how he'd acquired it for the next twenty-five minutes. Leila had to wonder if he'd been that boring when he and Farrah had met. Maybe Farrah had overlooked it out of sheer desperation. *Hmph.*

Their tour brought them around to where they'd started, where oversized paintings adorned the walls. It was the only place in the home with color. Tasteless, but at least it was a change from the lack of flavor. In the corner, an alabaster sculpture sat on a cherrywood stand, a near-perfect match to the twelve-seater table in the center. "And finally, the dining area. I was out one day antiquing and found this bust of Michigan's tenth governor, Andrew Parsons. I was pretty lucky to get it—"

"That's good, Stan. Now, can you take off your shirt and climb up on top of this lovely table?" Leila dragged her finger over the edge of the wood and pinned him with another intoxicating stare, literally.

"Oh, sure. That's no problem at all. Are you sure you don't want something to drink?"

Farrah took her boots off the table and sat forward, still the unwilling participant.

The legs shook, the wood crying out from Stan's weight as he got up, shirtless now.

"What is that?" Leila asked Farrah. She pointed to the pale-colored material that almost looked like an Ace bandage stretched around his midsection.

"Why, that's what they call a male girdle," Farrah admitted, the start of a smile appearing.

"Yes, it's my girdle. I wear it because I want to give the illusion that I work out like my dating profile says. But I don't. I hate sweating. So, instead, I wear this. If I sleep with anyone, I just turn the lights out, and no one is the wiser."

"Get the fuck outta here." Leila slapped her palm to her forehead.

"Okay," Stan said, sitting back up and preparing to get off the table.

"No, no. You stay right here, sweetie. We need you to be still, okay?" Leila pressed her palm into his chest and pushed him back down onto the tabletop.

When she was done, she looked over at Farrah and

motioned. Gesturing to his neck, Leila extended her fangs.

Farrah ran her finger across her throat, lips twisted toward Leila, the suggestion that she was going to kill her once all this was over.

"Okay, Stan. Now, you are going to feel the most intense pleasure of your life. Farrah and I are each going to bite you, me on your neck and her on your—"

"Wrist," Farrah chimed in. The desire to feed from his neck obviously gone, under the circumstances. Given his actions, Leila could hardly blame her.

"Yes, your wrist. Are you ready, honey?" Leila asked. She hated having to be so kind, but violence led to memories. Certain emotions left an impression that even the best of charms failed to conceal.

"Can't wait. Make sure it's very pleasurable," he responded, nearly squirming on the table.

"Oh, it will be." As Leila spoke to him, she held up her fingers, counting down from three. And then, they struck, both of them simultaneously. Stan vibrated, his cock straining against his pants. The top of his girdle, just like girdles do, rolled down off his fleshy belly and exposed the hairy skin. Leila closed her eyes, concentrating on the cinnamon-hinted blood that seeped into her mouth.

Asshole or not, his blood was delicious. Leila indulged while he grabbed hold of her head and fisted her hair in his hand, then pressed her into his flesh. His moans mingled in with Farrah's as they took from him. They didn't stop until Stan was jerking from what was probably the most forceful orgasm of his life.

Leila released him, knowing full well that between her and Farrah taking their meal from him, and him releasing a punchbowl of semen, he would need several days to recuperate.

"Damn," she snipped. "He may be a dick, but that was some high-quality plasma right there."

"You're so stupid," Farrah told her, a laugh rattling in her throat. Farrah ran her fingertip over her lips to catch some of the blood splashes and licked her finger clean. "Should we put him in the bed?"

"Nah."

Stan was coiled in the fetal position, his wounds already closing. He had placed his thumb in his mouth and was sucking for dear life.

"We just leave him here so when he wakes up in the morning, he thinks he had a wet dream alone on the dining room table?"

"Pretty much."

Leila put a sinister smirk on her face. Farrah smiled along with her. "All right, girl. I'm driving. C'mon, let's go."

"So, you still planning on opening this vampire matchmaking agency? It's a bit risky," Leila said as they rounded the corner and made their way to Farrah's car.

"I guess. I mean, what have I got to lose?"

"Everything. We have everything to lose. But if you do it, I support you. Just promise me you'll be careful."

Somehow, Leila knew no matter how careful they were, something was bound to go wrong. The question was, how long would they get away with it?

CHAPTER ONE

*L*eila stood there, staring at the man she didn't think she would ever have to confront again. He'd told her she was his lily, the beautiful flower he couldn't live without... but he'd lied, hadn't he?

Shifting away from him, she went over the reasons for not trusting him in her mind a thousand times. But in this case, she needed him. He was a requirement to save someone she loved so desperately. Farrah was more important to her than some petty moment between her and Mael.

Of course, it hadn't felt petty at the time. Long ago, she'd buried that part of herself. And now, with him back in the picture—for what seemed to be long-term—she would have to face the heartbreak still haunting her all these years later. It had taken half a century for her to stop turning over and reaching for him in the night. She would need a lifetime to forget him. Thankfully, as a vampire, she had many human lifetimes to practice.

"Leila, you wanna look at this?"

She wasn't sure how long Farah had been staring at

her. Nor was she sure what, exactly, she'd said moments before. "Yeah, of course." She blinked, bringing her thoughts back to the present. There were a million things to consider. One of Farrah's clients was still missing. Concerning, especially since she was one of the Order of Immortals members' daughters. Tarik was a pretty scary dude, from what Leila had heard. Presumably, Eire had been kidnapped by the hunters that Mael and Anwar had ended last month. But they had no idea where the humans had taken her.

Reluctantly, Leila approached the group of them as they hovered over an iPad while reviewing the traffic cam footage provided by the Order. It was a serious situation, which was the reason Leila didn't need to split her attention between the matter at hand and the fallen angel who'd broken her heart. "Anything so far?" She asked the question while avoiding Mael's all-too-frequent, lustful glances.

"You recognize this car?" Anwar asked. He was apparently an Atlantean warrior, a prince from the race that had spawned vampires. Leila supposed that meant she should thank him. But could she trust him with Farrah? Farrah was all she had left in the world, and Leila didn't want her to end up like her. With a stone for a heart. Leila was against mating but not against Farrah's happiness.

"I don't think so... Why?"

Anwar cast a questioning glance in Mael's direction.

"Because this guy, whoever he is, has been going to Melody for over a month. Night after night. Like he's searching for something. And—" Mael hit the touchscreen, bringing up another set of cameras. The building was one step away from demolition. A slim figure appeared, stalking the perimeter, aggression in every step. "This is the warehouse where they held you and Farrah the day before the shit went down. Seems to be a human, but I can't get a good view of his distinguishing features."

Melody was her place, and she couldn't stand the thought that someone had possibly used her bar to do harm to Farrah. "Hmph," Leila said, then leaned down to get a closer look. She still stopped by her club often, even if every night recently was spent at the Vintage Modernism Authority, otherwise known as the Vampire Matchmaking Agency, or the VMA by clients. Even with Anwar and Mael bird-dogging Melody, she wasn't quite ready to trust them with something she loved. Mael had already shown her who he was once. She didn't need a second lesson. "I haven't seen him. But I can run him by Mike, my regular bartender."

"I bet," Farrah said with a chuckle. She was attempting humor.

Leila had dabbled with Mike on one long-ago night, but that wasn't something she wanted to admit. Farrah had had some suspicions, of course. "Let it go, Elsa. I'll let you know what he says. Can you print me out a clearer image?" While she was asking Mael, she kept her eyes trained on Anwar. She couldn't risk the possibility of exposing herself, and her secret longing, to the bastard. Mael had her heart on a string, and any one tug might just implode the raggedy thing.

"I can do that," Mael piped up.

It was gridiron will that resisted the magnetic pull of his voice and kept her eyes trained on Anwar. Every word Mael spoke made her ache with need. The desire was only getting worse the more she was around him.

Once they found out who was behind the kidnappings that seemed targeted at the VMA, Leila would put a stop to seeing Mael's fine ass once and for all. "Fine," she replied, the icy edge in her voice serving as camouflage for the fire deep inside her. Goddamn him.

"Mael"—Anwar shifted his attention to her friend, but not before a sideways glance at Farrah—"we need to get over to the Order. Maybe Viktoria will be in a less murderous mood today."

While the Order was preoccupied with who could have been ballsy enough to take Tarik's daughter, they hadn't been focused on VMA and the fact that Farrah had blatantly violated the established accords. Leila hoped it would remain that way, indefinitely.

"Yeah, true that. See you later, ladies." A wicked smirk curled the corners of full lips. The deep voice combined with perfect gray eyes and a light brown complexion—Mael was the equivalent of a heavenly supermodel.

"I guess, or whatever." Leila tore her eyes away from him. She still remembered the silken-smooth caress of his wing feathers against her skin. He would cover them beneath their expanse simply because she loved the touch of them against her naked flesh.

"I'll see you tonight," Anwar said, then headed to Farrah and placed the gentlest kiss on her lips.

Granted, Leila didn't want to be mated, but how long had it been since she'd been kissed? The types of relationships she'd grown accustomed to were not the kind that involved lips. They were mostly fang-and-bear-it-type interludes. There was no envy of Farrah. But perhaps a touch of longing for someone to look at her that way... to hold her in the same regard.

Without another word, she headed into the VMA

lobby. The primary directive was to keep Farrah safe. That meant every night was spent at the VMA—and would be until they found out who was behind the kidnappings and had rescued Eire. To think, Eire, daughter of the faerie king, had been abducted by *humans*. The thought infuriated Leila.

Flopping down onto the blue velvet couch in the front of the store, she waited for Farrah to come up front with the same routine she'd fallen into for the past few weeks.

"You know," Farrah started, following the love of her relatively short life to the front of the store and watching him leave like she was going to crawl after him. Again, it wasn't jealously... right? "You don't have to stay here, Leila. I know you like your free time."

"I'm fine," she said before taking the cell from her pocket and opening her Instagram. "It's best if you have someone with you. I honestly don't want to have to go down this path again. So, let's just skip it tonight, shall we?"

"Oooowww, you are a bit surlier than usual. Wanna talk about it, sport?" The cushions of the antique leather couch Farrah sat on let out a bit of a squeak.

"Not particularly... Mother."

"I think every time you see Mael, you end up with a pole shoved straight up your ass for a few hours."

This was the comment that brought her head up. "I am completely unaffected by that shell of an angel and his snarky ass." With a slap, she brought the phone against her thigh, the sound coming out way louder than she expected. While it stung, she refused to let it show on her face. "By the way, I was physically assaulted less than a month ago, all because of my ties to VMA... presumably. I can't be a little on edge?" All of these were valid points, but it pissed Leila off to know she'd been outed. Farrah was seeing straight through what Leila thought was a fantastic façade.

"Um-hmm. I get it. However, you can't BS your way out of the evidence. And all signs point to Mael getting under your skin. Those little zone-out sessions whenever he's around? The avoiding eye contact with him? You don't even like Anwar that much, and you stare at him while talking to Mael."

"Oh my gawd, could it be that I abhor looking at the miscreant? He is repugnant—"

"Oh, girl. You've got it worse than Usher back in the day. Honey, you only use your fifty-cent words for people you can't stop thinking about."

"Shut up. Don't you have some appointments to get ready for?" It was a pitiful excuse for changing the topic, but when trapped in a corner, Leila would use what she had.

Farrah rolled her eyes and leaned back in her chair. "I do. Mr. Batchelor is still in need of a date. Can I tell you something, though?"

Clearly, her efforts had paid off. Picking up her phone, Leila resumed the human doom-scrolling. "Sure, what is it? Mr. Batchelor getting you down again?"

"Kind of. I'm a little afraid to set anyone else up. I've been dragging my feet on everyone since everything popped off. This isn't exactly a comforting time. I can't help but wonder whether it's one of my clients that's causing all the mischief."

Leila glanced up over the top of the phone. "And you think it would be Mr. Batchelor? He is older than time. Granted, he looks like a sixty-year-old human, but he seems too lonesome to be out here disregarding potential dates with perfectly viable females." To think someone of her own species could be so vile... vampires were a lot of things, but there was somewhat of an honor code between them. Sure, they were the largest group in the Order of Immortals, but there was still danger among the humans. And there were rules, either way.

"No... I mean... we shouldn't disregard anyone in this whole thing. And if we go to trial with the Order for existing in the first place, some things may turn up. I may as well be prepared just in case it is one of my clients... which would kind of mean it's my fault, right?"

Leila sat up to give Farrah her full attention. "There are a lot of things that we have done wrong over the courses of our lifetimes, but you were just trying to help everyone find love. No. It is definitely not your fault. You can't take responsibility for what happened—what may have happened—to anyone. Even if the victims weren't using VMA, they could have been ganked by hunters. Now, Ennis is working on identifying a link, and Anwar and Mael are combing through those recordings every day. Something will turn up, and we'll get Eire back. I don't even want to think of any other outcome. You can't, either."

Farrah was staring down at the floor but nodded her head in agreement.

Leila hoped her message got through to her because she wouldn't be able to keep the faith for both of them. She was having a hard enough time of it on her own.

CHAPTER TWO

As they waited for their time before the Order, Mael's mind was a thousand miles away. Across town with Leila was closer to accurate. She was growing increasingly distant. There were days in the beginning that she hadn't sneered at him. Now, she wouldn't even look at him without appearing as if she were going to spit.

"These fuckers get on my nerves, Mael. I think they keep us waiting for the sake of putting us in our places."

Mael grunted in agreement.

"You all right, my brother?"

Another thing he was growing tired of was lying to Anwar about what Viktoria had been up to. It was challenging not telling Anwar all he knew every day, but the worst was betraying their friendship. A sinking in his gut at the mere thought of it told him he was probably dying a little inside as each second passed. "Yeah, I'm fine. I'm just frustrated that we need to deal with these clowns at all. They won't lift a finger to help. You'd think Tarik wasn't concerned about his daughter in the slightest, since he practically dismissed us."

"Don't even bring that shit up, Mael. He makes me want to throttle him with his condescending tone."

"Yeah... well, Tarik would fuck around and find out." Mael completed his latest circle around the vestibule and stopped in front of Anwar, who was sitting on the marble slab in the center of the room. It was an ascetic setting, but Anwar, with his unconscious royal demeanor, classed the place up a bit. Though his family wore none of their regalia, he still seemed as if he was outfitted to the nines. "This is all for show, you know?"

"Yeah, I do. But since they haven't enforced a single law in decades, I can't see them doing anything about VMA, or me either, for that matter."

The ache in the center of his chest flared up again as Anwar spoke. He knew what Viktoria, the head member of the Order, had up her sleeve from firsthand knowledge. What she was waiting on to spring the news, Mael had no idea. In the end, the VMA had been outed due to what the hunters had done and not actually what Mael had told her. But it still stung like a sonofabitch to have been in cahoots with her at all.

Mael didn't reply to Anwar, choosing instead to finish his pacing around the sparsely decorated space.

The sound of the door creaking open halted his footsteps. Leave it to the Order to make shit radically uncomfortable just because they could. The armed guards were new and had been added as a security measure until things got back to normal.

Two of the tallest shifters Mael had ever laid eyes on stood at the entrance like soldiers. Clad in black, close-cut camo, they could have easily been a pair of wrestlers the humans watched on Mondays. As he and Anwar passed through, Mael could smell their apprehension. Undoubtedly, they'd been warned to be wary of them—a fallen angel and an Atlantean. It would take more than a couple of shifters to hold them at bay if shit went left. If it did, though, and if he had mere moments remaining in the world, he was glad to be doing something that meant a lot to Leila. Farrah was someone important to her, and as such, she was important to him. Even if Anwar hadn't been in the picture.

"Well, if it isn't the Hardy Boys come back from their latest mystery. Tell us, what misadventure have you been on this time?" Viktoria shifted her stance, her hair a stark blond departure from the coal black color a week prior.

"We are close to something. We have a male of interest, and—"

"Anwar, we aren't seeking someone of interest. We want the human responsible. That Billy McDermott person you dug up recently... What of him?" Tarik had no problem butting in, of late.

"He has gone underground, it seems," Mael piped up, unable to hold his tongue. The truth was, Mael was a couple inches off Tarik's ass. The king of the fae had been intent on asserting his dominance. "It doesn't help that we have to return here almost nightly to report our comings and goings. It seems like overkill."

Viktoria's brows popped nearly into her bleached hairline. "Is that so? We seem to be bothering you, Maelstrom. Perhaps there are things you'd like to get off your chest?"

She was toying with him. In order to protect his brother, Mael had sworn to look after Lelania, the Nephilim child he'd tried his best to hide from the world. The angels would kill her if they knew she existed. He'd been cloaking her signal for years. And had done a fan-fucking-tastic job of it until Viktoria had uncovered his secret and began forcing him to spy on Anwar.

"I only mean to say that we are losing time. Perhaps we might relay information to you via text?"

The heat of nearly every Order member was upon him. As a fallen angel, he could sense emotions. Knew that they would love to kill him for his insolence. "No, we would have you come here, as requested. At our leisure. Is that perfectly understood?" Viktoria barked.

Mael had to practically bite his tongue to keep from snapping her head off. Images of first Leila, then Lelania, blazed a lightning trail through his mind. They were the most important. They were worth saving. He pressed against the cage of his gritted teeth and held back the barrage of curse words. But one day, Viktoria would get what she had coming to her.

"I'll take your silence as acquiescence. Since there is no news of the assailants, that will be all, for now. You are both dismissed," she said, her voice like nails scraping over steel in Mael's mind.

Anwar was the first to turn away to head from the room. Mael took a few steps facing the Order members, primarily because he didn't trust them as far as he could spit. They weren't worth the designer clothing they wore —most of them, anyway—and with so much animosity radiating from their persons, he knew it would be wise to keep his gaze trained on them.

As he turned away, he glared at Tarik. He was the one who would most likely try something. A part of Mael itched to take his head off. Alas, it would not be today.

Tarik leaned against the wall, glowering down at Mael from his normal position. He didn't move a muscle, though. Just stared. It wasn't fear that held him off. He was calculating, working out some plan in his mind. Though Mael couldn't read whatever emotion Tarik was struggling to conceal, he knew beyond a shadow of a doubt it wasn't good news for VMA, for Farrah, Anwar, and by association, him and Leila, either.

From that moment on, they would need to watch their backs even more than they had before.

CHAPTER THREE

FARRAH

At any minute, Anwar would be walking through the door. Her door. It was hard to believe she'd gotten so lucky and met him in the first place. While they hadn't completed their blood mating by simultaneously exchanging blood, he was very much a part of her. Everything she wanted in one tall, fascinatingly gorgeous package—not to mention the way he loved her. More than physical. It was mental, metaphysical, and all-consuming. If she were a poet, he would be her muse.

After finally kicking Leila—who had become somewhat of a helicopter liege—out, she was putting the finishing touches on her look for the night. Dressing up in scanty lingerie wasn't something Anwar expected of her, but Farrah loved the hungry look in his eyes whenever she did. Tonight, she wore a black lace number, nearly transparent except for strategically placed roses to cover up her naughty bits.

Her phone rang as soon as she put on her favorite deep red lipstick. She sprinted at top speed to get the phone before it rang a second time, though she knew it was probably Anwar. Being a vampire had some advantages, after all.

Grabbing her cell from the circular coffee table, she didn't bother to check the screen before she answered. "Hey, baby."

"Hey, yourself."

The moment the words were uttered, a frigid chill ran the length of her spine. In that moment, she was keenly aware that this was definitely not Anwar. *Dammit...* "Who is this?" She asked the question knowing full well whoever it was wouldn't reveal their identity.

"I hope you aren't dressing up for me, gorgeous. We won't meet for a little while still. But just know, I'm watching you. And waiting..." The laugh was gravelly, hard, and coarse. The mystery voice crawled all over her flesh, leaving her raw and bleeding from the contact.

"I'm not afraid of you," she said, more for herself than for whoever the bastard was on the other end. She needed to believe it if she was going to keep him on the phone long enough for a trace. Ennis, the VMA tech genius, had wired all the lines to trace inbound and outbound calls. They had always known the battle wasn't over. The call was what they needed if they ever wanted to see Eire again, yet exactly what they feared.

"You don't have to be now. But I promise you, as I watch the light die from your eyes, you will be. Until then..."

"Wait," she shouted. "What do you want?" It was too late, however. The line went dead, and as she looked at the receiver, the screen read *call failed*. "Fuck." There was nobody there to curse to or at, and the knowledge made the forceful chill from moments earlier return.

While sprinting around her apartment to check the windows and doors, she called Anwar. With shaky hands, she disengaged and re-engaged the locks, her eyes burning with tears she wouldn't let fall.

"Hey sweetheart, I'm—"

"Anwar... he called."

There was a moment of silence on the line, and it was as if she could feel tension radiating through the receiver. "I'm on my way. Did you lock down the apartment?"

"I did just now," she said.

"I want you to go to the closet, and beneath your shoe boxes, there is a small door. Go there now."

Farrah wouldn't allow herself to hesitate. She reacted, having been warned about the potential for danger all around her. She knew if something were to pop off, she would only have moments to react. If the last few weeks had taught her anything, relaxing into a sense of safety was ill-advised, to say the least.

The sprint down the hallway was a lightning-fast motion. Along the way, she felt a pinch in her bare foot but didn't stop to check what it was. There was no slowing down until she was in the closet on hands and knees. "Okay..."

"Open it," he said, his voice steely and firm. She could hear the rush of wind and movement, comforting her as she knew he was on his way to her side.

The nearly imperceptible slot made level with the hardwood gave as she pressed into the wall. Every instruction from Anwar's earlier preparedness training rang in her mind. As he said the words, she was already moving, grabbing the handle of the blade, a smooth steel surface that felt alien in her hands. She hadn't been one to carry weapons in the past, but these days, Farrah was getting more and more comfortable. The mini sword she pulled out was the weapon of choice since guns couldn't kill supernaturals all the time, but a knife could take them and humans out if used correctly. Better safe than sorry considering they didn't know what exactly they were dealing with.

"Got it," she said, slipping into the closet and pulling the false back in front of her. It was a hiding spot, and while it wouldn't necessarily save her if someone should dig deeper into her closet, it was intended to give Anwar or Mael time to get to her. With her back against the cool wall, she waited.

"Listen to me. Do not leave, do you understand?" Anwar was panting, something that was uncommon for him. He was impossibly athletic and had been training for weeks with Mael... just in case, he'd said.

"Um-hmm," Farrah said. Fear stripped her of her ability to form logical sentences. She was half listening in case someone was breaking into her apartment. Farrah should have stayed with Leila like she'd been urging her to. Or at Anwar's, since he lived so close to the Order's headquarters.

"I'm coming up the alley," he said.

Just the thought of him being in her immediate vicinity calmed her a bit more. Before she could breathe easy, she heard it. There was a sound in the living room, like splintering wood. "Anwar, is that you?"

"No. Be still, I will be in there in seconds. Don't make a sound," he said.

And she didn't. The cell phone cut into her hand where she gripped it tightly as she waited. There were noises near the front of the apartment, but she couldn't tell if they were coming or going. Between near-silent panting and trying to still her shivers, she heard the redirection of footsteps—unsure where they were going, she only knew they grew closer.

If she needed her heart to beat or her breath to provide life-sustaining oxygen, it would have been her end.

Clomp, clomp, clomp. Heavy footfalls were in the same room with her, and she didn't dare scream out Anwar's name, nor move, nor make a single sound as she waited in the too-small panic room. In another moment, shattered glass interrupted the sound of footsteps. Then running.

A shuffling noise was just outside the closet, and Anwar may not arrive in time to help her. He would need time to get there. He couldn't very well teleport. She heard the movement on the phone. On the way... he was still en route to her location. What if she was right? Mael wouldn't make it in time, and there would be no one to save her.

Something about the internal question gave her newfound resolve. Steeling herself, she gripped the handle of the blade tighter and pressed the phone closer to her face. Someone sane would have put the damned thing down, but Farrah wanted to be able to use her last breath to tell him she loved him, no matter how short a time they'd been together.

The door of the closet opened wide, and light spilled beneath the fake wall. A quick inhale told her it was a male, pheromones scenting the air. Whoever it was didn't smell remotely human.

Pressing back into the wall, she held the blade

outward, ready to launch forward. Unable to stand it anymore, she whispered, "Anwar... they found me."

In another blink, the door was ripped away from her hiding space, and she blinked into the light. She squeezed her eyes shut, then with all the power in her legs, she pushed herself up and out, sword extended.

To her surprise, she didn't hit flesh and bone. Instead, the sword was pulled from her hand, and she was wrapped in a tight embrace. "Oh my God, I thought—"

Every bit of tension seeped from her as she recognized the voice, but not his scent. "Anwar," she whispered. There were no other words as she dissolved into tears, collapsing into his arms and allowing herself to be swept away as he folded her into his large body.

"Farrah, are you hurt? Did they..."

"No, no... no..." she babbled. There was no way to make herself coherent. Not in that moment. She'd thought... she had been sure, rather, that everyone's luck ran out eventually. There was no way she would make it out of that situation fresh off two prior near-death experiences. Dying the first time had sucked. The next time would surely be more permanent.

"I've got you... I'm here," Anwar said, his lips pressed into her hair.

She dropped the cell phone without a care to where it fell and strung her arms around his neck. He was the only thing she wanted to touch, to feel, in that moment. "I thought... I didn't know—" Hiccupping sobs chopped her sentence into a million unintelligible syllables.

"It's okay." Anwar continued the trek to wherever. It felt too far to be her bed, but with her head buried in his neck, she couldn't see. Nor did she care, as long as he was there.

In another moment, he lowered her down and pulled away from her as she spilled onto the soft surface. With one glance around, she knew he'd brought her to the living room. "Someone was here. I heard them outside the door, and when the glass broke, there was running."

"I know. I could sense a presence, then it was gone before I could catch them." He tried to stand from his kneeling position in front of her, but she grabbed at him to keep him there. "I just need to check the door, okay?"

She knew her eyes were too wide as she tried to nod, still shaky from the ordeal.

"I'll be right back," he said.

Farrah watched as he went through every nook and cranny of her place, ensuring they were safe. He was back in a moment that felt too long. "What did they want, Anwar?"

He stood there, hands on his hips and chest heaving, with a look of frustration twisted into his steel-tight jawline. "I don't know... whatever it was, it doesn't look like they got it."

"Okay. I was so scared..."

"Don't worry. We're going to find that bastard," he said, taking a seat next to her on the couch.

Even before he put his massive arm around her, Farrah moved forward and folded into the crook of his elbow, his warmth and strength acting as her personal safety net. She inhaled, taking in the scent of him. "What is that smell?" she asked. It wasn't quite unpleasant, but it was different. He normally smelled of pine and sandalwood, fresh like an autumn day. But now, it was closer to spice and cloves.

"That is part of my *kensee*... When someone we... we love is in danger, or before we go into battle, it smells different. Each scent varies for every male. Mine is unique to my own biochemical signature."

"You make it sound like a chemistry experiment," she said, her sense of humor having survived her momentary breakdown.

"Yes, well... it's not like I've ever smelled it before. It's... well, you see, normally, mated males of my species have a different scent. And you and I aren't... we haven't yet..."

As Anwar struggled to get the words out, as much as Farrah wanted to take back all the caution she'd placed on their mating, the ritual only to be completed once they were sure, she began to regret them. She wanted to be his. But it wasn't the right time to tell him that, was it?

The truth of the matter was, as much as she wanted to lay claim to Anwar, she wanted it to be as much her choice as it was his. With the difficulty he had in getting out that last sentence, perhaps he wasn't ready.

"It's okay. I'm still..." She swallowed hard. "I didn't know who you were when you found me in the closet."

"Yes, and I should have told you about it. I didn't have the chance with everything going on. But, let's not worry about that now. Let me hold you for a moment. I'll have to call Mael soon, but I need to get my anger under control. Do you mind?" he asked, pulling her impossibly closer to his body.

"No... I don't mind at all." She allowed herself to be scooped onto his lap and leaned into him, resting her head on his shoulder. Mating, as important a discussion as it should have been, took a back seat for the moment. Farrah just wanted to let him hold her. He made her feel safe and needed. That would have to be fine for now.

CHAPTER FOUR

*M*ael felt like a fool standing outside Melody, longing for someone he could never have. Only a few weeks prior, he'd headed into the club and found out it belonged to Leila, and now, his nerves tightened in his gut with just the thought of passing through those doors again.

The weather was changing, and he could feel the cool undercurrent in the wind off the Detroit River. Mael pulled his black leather jacket closer to his body, warding off the chill. Heaven was a warm place, and no matter how many years he'd been on Earth, he never got used to its seasons. Especially in a place like Michigan.

In fact, he'd never been as warm as when he'd had Leila in his arms.

It had only been a month or so since she'd been back in his life, but not touching her was becoming more of a burden than he'd anticipated.

He had a perfect excuse for being outside her establishment. He was waiting for the man they'd identified in the traffic cam footage to show his ugly mug, but the task of not going into that bar and dragging her out was the most challenging thing he'd ever done. He felt like an asshole skulking around. While she knew he was there, she'd insisted he keep out of her sight. As difficult as it had been, he was making it happen. He would only engage if absolutely necessary. As a result, he planned to circle the perimeter until she was no longer on the premises.

Was it stupid to feel so good when she berated him with that oh-so-sweet, foul mouth of hers? Yes. But at least she was speaking to him. Her silence around him felt far worse than her terse words.

Mael shook his head as he rounded the corner once more. Melody had been a former warehouse and was customary Detroit design—exposed brick walls and open space inside, deep cranberry-colored brick with paned windows as tall as they were wide in turn-of-the-nineteenth-century architecture. Most buildings of its kind had been demolished or sat being chipped away beneath the brunt of winter snow and the elements. But Melody had been remodeled with Leila's own elegant fingers.

This trip around, Mael looked in through the window and saw Leila laughing with the shifty human they called Mike. It took every ounce of his will to keep from charging in and liberating the bartender's head from its piddly neck. "Asshole," Mael whispered to no one in particular.

He glanced up in time to find another human walking past. The man stared at him a little weirdly, and Mael wasn't sure whether it was because he'd been caught talking to himself or because he looked like a madman. Most likely the latter.

"'S'cuse me, brother," he said, adapting his speech pattern to make it more like he looked—a Black guy, mid-twenties, from Detroit, when in actuality, he was an eons-old angel. Falling from grace should have been the worst thing in his life. But it wasn't. It had been losing Leila. And if he had to walk the earth for a million more years, he was sure he would never ache so badly for another female. For anything.

When the cell phone vibrated in his jacket pocket, he pulled it out with a curse. The only one to ever call him was Anwar. And if he was calling no more than an hour after going to his female, something was desperately wrong.

"What's up?" Mael said into the receiver as he brought the phone to his ear.

"It's Farrah. Someone came for her tonight. Can't figure out how they got in, but they were definitely here. Any sign of that dude? I've got a feeling it may have been him but can't be sure without footage."

"Nah, no sign of him. He'll turn up, though. Be we should have known they would try something sooner or later... You could've installed that camera at her place like I told you. That is, since she won't stay at your place like you told her."

"Farrah is not exactly the do-as-I-say type, you know."

Mael heard Farrah's voice come through the line saying something like, "Damn straight."

"Well, get that call log from Ennis. I'll go in and let Leila know."

"You haven't been inside yet?"

He could hear the sarcasm in Anwar's tone. Damn him. He knew Mael was walking on eggshells around Leila. "Never mind that. I'm going in now."

"All right. Let her know that I'm taking Farrah home

with me for the day. We'll lockdown there and meet up again at dusk. Cool?"

"Yup." Mael hit the end call button onscreen before slipping the phone back into his pocket.

He took a deep sigh before walking into the bar. He needed to gird himself each time he went in to talk to her because all his instincts urged him to grab her and make love to her right where she stood. They were old-school, barbarian-type urges he had to contend with, but damned if he could help himself.

The door swung open, and as Mael stepped over the threshold, it was as if Leila knew the second his foot landed in her stratosphere. Through slitted eyes, she stared at him on his approach. He could see the hatred in them. And, in more recent days, he could tell she was not warming up to him. In fact, the closer he got tonight, as he dogged the mass of humans dancing, drinking, and cavorting beneath the purple and red lights of the club, he could swear she wanted to murder him. Her eyes were daggers of ice and pain, and he wanted so badly to erase every bit of the sorrow he'd caused her. She had been the best thing to ever happen to him, and she had been too good for him before he broke her heart. He damned sure didn't deserve her now. Not a moment's worry, not a single tear. He knew it. And it was his cross to bear.

"Leila," he said as he stepped forward, crossing the last few inches to her seat at the bar.

"Fucker," she said, an acrid smile on her lips.

Fuck if his cock didn't stir. He was surely a goddamned masochist. "We need to talk. Something's happened." He watched as a veil of worry slipped into place over her features.

"Aye, you all right, Leila?" the cock-sucking bartender Mike asked.

Mael did his best to keep from strangling the fucker by shoving his hands into his pockets. "Yeah, we're good, thanks. I'll call you if I need a drink. Got me?"

Much to his credit, Mike didn't run away and cower. Instead, he stared back. "I was talking to Leila. Not you. And if she so much as utters the words *angel shot*, I'm bouncing your lanky ass up out of here. You got me?"

He had to look behind him to see who the little man was referencing because Mael knew for damned sure he wasn't lanky.

"I got it, Mike. Thank you. I'll be back in a moment." She gave him a weak smile before sliding off her stool. "Come with me, Mael."

Stepping back, he allowed her to pass and lead the way. He didn't move before tossing his most menacing archangel glare at Magic Mike, the little bastard. To which Mike made the popular human gesture with his middle finger. "Yeah, fuck you too," he said before turning and following Leila into the back space of the club.

The hallway honestly felt smaller than he'd expected. Or maybe that was the effect she had on him. Whenever he was near her, he was awkward and clumsy, too big of a body in spaces that grew ever tighter and more confining —everything from the walls to his clothes seemed to crash in on him. He was a mess, putting it mildly. Unfortunately, there was nothing to pull him out of his misery. While he had been in service to Anwar and his father, Constantine, for what seemed like eons, as was required of the fallen—to be of use to all God's creatures in penance for their sins—he would have to leave and find somewhere else to live out his days. There was no way he could maintain the torture of being in her proximity without having Leila in his arms. Moot point, really, since he had actively worked to betray Anwar. It seemed to be a trend because he'd let down everyone he'd ever loved.

"Come in," she said, her tone tipped in equal parts frigidity and concern. Her lithe body moved to the side, allowing him to pass. She wore a tank-style shirt made of mesh with a nearly see-through bra in black and silver beneath. Miles-long legs were encased in black leather, skintight and taunting Mael with her every movement.

"Thank you," he said, happy to be heading for the seat across the room since his manhood was ready to leap out and take matters into its own one-eyed hands... so to speak.

Though he didn't turn to watch her close the door and head to her desk inches before him, the damned windows picked up her reflection in the dim yellow glow of her office's natural lighting. It gave him a floor show of her fluid, sensual movements, and he remembered reaching out for her in those good old days. There was a time when he spent the whole of his time laboring over her body, giving her hours and hours of orgasms using nothing more than his mouth and hands, when his needs were secondary to the pleasure of hearing his name fall from her lips again and again... and again.

Before her luscious ass was even in the chair, she started in on him. Somewhere between the bar and walking to her office, she'd slipped her guard into place. The brief moment of interest in what he had to say and concern over the ongoing situation morphed into a realization that she needed to protect herself. From him. He could feel it, a wall between them. And there wasn't a damned thing he could do to break it down.

"Mael, this had better not be bullshi—"

"No, no. It's Farrah. She's okay, but someone came for her tonight. Anwar is with her. But I fear this is escalating. We're going to have to increase our efforts. In all the years I've known Anwar, I've never seen him like this. If something were to happen to your girl, he wouldn't be easy to piece together again."

With a sigh, she leaned back into her chair, the fabric a crimson so deep it reminded him of the blood rivulets that had spilled from her lips as she fed from him.

Dammit, he would have to stay out of the past. At the moment, she hated him. No sense in pretending. "I don't know if she would be able to take losing him, either." She shook her head, the blunt, straight ends slipping back and forth over her shoulders. "So, what's the plan?"

"Right now? Just to keep an eye on you and her to see if this Billy McDermott shows himself. He and the male who comes in all the time could be one and the same. I don't know if he's solely responsible, but he knows something. And we're going to have to find him."

"Okay. I came here after leaving Farrah at her apartment and checking in at VMA. Nobody showed in here tonight. I have the bouncers keeping an eye on things. If they saw him, I would know."

"Your boy Mike out there seems serious enough about the job." Mael tried to ease the hint of jealousy in his tone, but keeping his hands to himself was far easier than controlling his tongue.

"My employees and their enthusiasm aren't any of your concern, now, are they?" With a daggered stare, she practically nailed him to his seat.

"All that can change... all you have to do is ask."

"Mael, I'm not going to do this with you."

"Do what? Talk about me being under your command with a single word?" This time, he didn't use humor to temper their conversation. She needed to know. He wanted her to fully understand that if she were willing to give him a chance, he would do anything. Everything.

"So you say..."

"I do."

"It's too late, Mael. I tried the whole girlfriend/boyfriend thing. Shit doesn't work for me. I'm not one who likes being walked out on."

"Nor did I want to walk out on you. My brother needed me. But I don't have that problem anymore."

"What about Anwar?"

"What about him? He would never put unnecessary demands on me. But wait a minute... are you considering? Is that what we're doing? I don't want to push you, Leila. Fuck, I don't. But if you are—"

"I am most definitely not considering being your mate again."

"Okay... so you enjoy torturing me then?"

That brought a smile to her lips. Not one that was forced or tight. Natural. Her bright teeth, dangerous fangs on display. When had her fangs come out? He couldn't care fucking less. All Mael wanted was for her to keep looking just like that. "I don't get down like that, and you know it."

"I don't know. You used to be into all kinds of things. Remember?"

"Yeah. I remember. And look where it got me."

Dammit. He'd gone too far with trying to get back down memory lane. "I didn't mean to hurt you, Lily..."

"Don't call me that."

"That's right. Too close, isn't it?"

"Okay, that's enough. Why don't you pack up your marbles and get the fuck outta here?" She stood from her seat, smoothing her hands down pants that didn't need it.

"I'll go, sure. But that won't strip me from your mind. It won't erase the things we shared, Lily. You were mine and I was yours for a time. I fucked up. Even more so, since I ended up falling from grace anyway, but I want you to know."

"That's it, I'm out," she said, throwing her hands to the sides and allowing them to slap against her thighs as she moved from behind her desk.

"I want..." And as she kept walking, Mael knew he'd lost the internal battle to restrain himself with one movement across the floor. His hand grasped her elbow and pulled her around until she faced him. "I need you to know that my heart is in one of those fucking purses you own, smashed into a thousand pieces."

Her eyes, normally the color of hot whiskey, turned ice blue as she narrowed them, trained on his. "You sonofabitch. How dare you come back after all this time with this. You ruined me. Fucking destroyed me and didn't look back. You *remember that?*"

"I do. It was like a million lifetimes until I could stop following you around, hopping from rooftop to rooftop as you drove around this dismal-ass city. I stayed away. Seventy-five years, I've stayed away, Lily. You—"

"I've asked you not to call me that," she snapped, right before he felt the cool wind across his face.

It was a few moments before he felt the sting. And there it was, his cock ready to burst through the stiff denim of his jeans. "Do it again, and I swear you'll regret it... *Lily.*"

Leila snatched away from him, bringing her hand up

and slapping him again. The coppery taste of blood filled his mouth and his lips went numb on the side she'd smacked. Mael swiped at swollen lips and wiped the blood away. He had a mind to take her, right there on the floor. To spill himself inside her until she could barely walk. But... but, he didn't. He had done enough, truly.

Once more, he bore down on his growing urge to take her and stepped away.

"I thought you were going to make me pay, Mael? Yet another promise you can't keep." Before he could reply, she stepped into him.

Anger fucking never resolved anything, but as she pressed the mouth he'd dreamed of for nearly a century against his, damned if he could resist her. With his still-bloody hand, he stroked her cheek gently before running his palm around her neck and pressing her into him, closer, deeper.

As their kiss grew more powerful, more consuming, he felt her fingers run up his back beneath his shirt, then hissed as her nails dragged over his flesh, breaking open skin and ripping the Band-Aid off ancient wounds in his heart. "Fuck, I want you," he whispered against her mouth.

"Take me, then," she said, biting into the soft flesh of his lip. She suckled him, her mouth drawing out his life force. The sensation was so arousing, even if she drained him dry, he would have been helpless to do anything.

He hissed as the sting of her fangs teetered on the borderline of pain. Sweet fuck help him, but he scented her arousal, forcing desire so strong, his vision went checkerboard for a moment. "You sure, Lily? Because if I start..." He pulled his lip from her fang, only serving to tear the delicate flesh.

"Don't do that, Mael... I don't fuck around with what I want. You, of all people, know that I don't turn my back on the things I see."

Standing there, with his cock rock hard, her ice-blue stare ripping him to shreds, and her lips tinged red from his blood, though her words stabbed another hole into his heart, he was ready. He didn't care. She could tear him apart so badly he could never recover, and he wouldn't say no. Not to her. Not ever again.

CHAPTER FIVE

It was a piss-poor idea. But she let him rip her pants from her body.

The worst thing she could possibly do was let him make her feel the way he used to, but she couldn't stop herself. Didn't want to stop it from happening.

He lifted her savagely and rested her bare ass on the smooth, lacquered desk. A trail of blood from his injured mouth ran down her belly as he kissed his way to her core. Using her fingers, she swiped at the sweetest elixir she'd ever tasted. The moment she stuck her middle finger into her mouth, he latched on to her pussy, his expert tongue laving over her clit and bathing her in the glow of ecstasy.

Capable hands clutched her thighs and spread her as he feasted on the most sensitive places. "Let me touch them," she moaned.

It was the only time he paused, a slight hesitation as her request landed in the tiny space between their bodies. Rising to his full height, he took the jacket off, then labored over the buttons of his white shirt.

After what felt like an eternity, he stripped the cotton material free and unfurled the most glorious of wings. An expanse from tip to tip of no less than seven feet, arched high in the confines of her office and filling the room with their splendor.

Her fangs tingled with the urge to sink into his flesh once more. She wanted him. Leila needed to take every part of him inside her at that moment.

She leaned forward, running both hands over the patagium, one on each side of the feather-coated boning that anchored them to his body. A growl escaped him as her fingertips danced over the intricate webbing. He'd told her once that her touching them was like a kiss over foreskin, nearly unbearable in the pleasure.

In the darkest parts of her soul, she was enjoying having such control over him, and she couldn't help but take advantage... just the tiniest bit. "Get on your knees, Mael."

Holding her stare without a single word, he complied with her demand. Dropping to his knees, he surrendered himself to her.

Leila leaned back on the desk, resting on her hands, and lifted her legs, then hooked them over his shoulders. Her bare feet slipped between the folds of his feathers, and she used them to pull his mouth back to her center.

Breaking the stare because she couldn't take it anymore, whether she wanted to admit it or not, she rolled her eyes up to the ceiling. As if on command, his mouth was on her again, kissing his way up her thighs before ministering over her pussy once more. Every part of her hummed to life, and she remembered everything she'd worked so hard to forget. The ache inside her that kept her awake all hours of the day. The desperate yearning for his touch when he was thousands of miles away from this place.

She whispered his name while at the same time forbidding her heart to feel anything.

The knock on the door pulled her away from the cliff she was nearly over. "Yeah," she cried out.

"Boss, I think you need to see this guy. I think it's the one." It was Drew. He was a police officer by day, trained in identifying people who didn't necessarily want to be seen.

"All right, I'll be out in a second," she said.

Mael pressed forward, as if willing her to go back to the place she had been seconds before. But she couldn't, right?

His tongue dove deeper, lapping at her tight entrance. "Mael, we have to stop," she said. Her mind knew it was true, but her body... Oh God, she wanted him to keep going. It was crazy, though... wasn't it?

No, no, she was in control. She had to be.

"Mael," she said, more forcefully than she'd intended.

It got his attention, but she could tell he was reluctant. She leaned up in time to catch the tender kiss he gave her sex.

"Yeah, I know," he said.

In an instant, Leila remembered herself. Turning to the side as he got to his feet, she swiped at the tears that had somehow fallen. "There's a bathroom over there," she said with a sniff.

"Nah. I'm good. I've been dreaming of your scent and the taste of your pussy for decades. I'm not washing that off anytime soon, Lily."

Lily. It had been his pet name for her. It still sent shivers all through her entire body. "Funny," she said.

"Except I'm not joking." His voice took on a sinister growl.

Again, she tried to deflect the tingles she felt every time she was around him. There was no way she would forget him if she didn't put a pin in it once and for all. Like she'd thought initially, it had been a bad fucking idea. "Look, Mael, I don't want you getting any wild thoughts. We will never be what we were. But... thanks for scratching that itch of mine." Yes, she knew it was wrong to let him believe she felt nothing, but he'd been wrong first. He'd walked out on her, after all.

She heard the snort as she bent over to pick up her pants.

"Yeah... happy to oblige," he said.

The pair of them dressed in silence. Leila couldn't say anything while she felt like this. While her body was alive and sensitive, longing for his touch. She still tasted his blood, the coppery sweetness lingering on her tongue reminding her of her solemn vow to never indulge in Mael again. The one she'd willingly broken in a moment of weakness.

"Oh, and just a warning. If that fucking bartender says one goddamned thing to me for the rest of the night, you're gonna find yourself short a staff member."

The sheer force and anger in his words brought her head around to find him snatching on his jacket over an open shirt. He didn't wait for a reply before storming from the office. He swung the door open and found Drew standing there. "Get out of my way, man," he barked, then shoved by, effectively removing the four-hundred-pound former linebacker from his path.

Leila wasn't a mind-reader of supernaturals, but something told her she'd perhaps lit a fuse no one was ready for. The problem... she wasn't sure which of them was going to blow first.

CHAPTER SIX

ANWAR

"*Y*ou've got to have your cockblocking radar on, Mael." Anwar struggled with going to find his dear friend and ripping every one of those feathers from his spine.

"Yeah, tell me about it."

"What?" He'd known Mael for nearly seventy years, and he'd never seen him care for a female. The way he behaved with Leila was different, and Anwar was concerned for his friend. Certain things were off-limits with friends, though. He wouldn't broach the subject unless Mael wanted to talk about it.

"Nothing. Look, he showed up at Melody. I'm following him. You stay put. I'm already going to have to deal with Leila wanting to tag along. I don't want that shit from both of them."

By both of them, Anwar assumed he meant Farrah, who had just rolled over. Great, Anwar was going to have to let her rest. She'd been so stressed, and the phone call had interrupted a blue-ball-inducing kissing session. "I'm going to try to talk her out of it. At least that'll be one out of the way. You deal with your *girl*."

"Oh, you're funny. Do that. I'll call you if anything comes up."

The call ended before Anwar could add anything on. It didn't take rocket science to know Mael was practically frosty. And while his demeanor hadn't exactly changed before tonight, he had been somewhat distant for months. Anwar hadn't wanted to pry, but he might have to break bro-code and do the unthinkable. Which was to ask how his friend was feeling.

"Who was that? Mael?"

"Yeah." He rolled over and gathered his female into his chest. "He thinks he's found something. But he'll call us back if necessary." He planted a kiss on her forehead. *His female...* It would take some time to get used to it, and it was a tremendous departure from what he'd thought he wanted. What he'd thought he deserved just a month earlier. Farrah was slowly becoming his everything. And he'd just lied to her. But he wanted her to rest. There was no way he was going to let her, or her stubborn-ass maker, walk into a dangerous situation. He'd seen Farrah nearly killed three times since he'd met her. There was no way he was going to risk that once again.

"Okay."

Against his chest, he felt her blow out warm air and shudder against him. "What's on your mind, baby girl?"

"It's just that I don't know if this will ever be over. And I have clients out there hanging. Waiting to meet their mate. I'm holding them up."

He couldn't help but chuckle. Wasn't that just like

her? "You're worried about your clients? I just carried you out of your apartment because someone threatened you tonight. We'll get to your clients. After you're safe. How about we take that approach?"

"Anwar, I refuse to allow them to scare me away from my work. I know they're dangerous. But I know how to protect myself now."

"You charged out of a closet, eyes shut tight, and was disarmed in less than two seconds. I think you may need a bit more practice."

"Yeah. I was unarmed by a million-year-old Atlantean. That's not on me. If you were human, you would have been dead. D.E.D. Trust." She lifted her head and stared Anwar straight in the eyes. "And mind you, I'm stronger than most human men."

"And if it hadn't been a human man? I hate to tell you that humans are the weakest and most helpless. We don't know what we're dealing with. They got in without even using the locks. There aren't many creatures capable of such a thing. And I can assure you, they aren't anywhere near weak as a man."

"Um-hmm, that remains to be seen. But if you insist, I'll do some more training with Mael."

"Yes, I'm afraid I do, my love."

"Fine. But I just want you to know it's overkill."

"I know, Xena. Overkill, but it would make me feel so much better, thank you very much."

"Xena," she said, resting her chin on his chest and staring up at him with eyes so warm they heated his soul.

Every time she looked at him, he found another thing to love about her. Right then, he saw a light path of freckles over the bridge of her nose. She usually wore what she called *tinted moisturizer* to get rid of the "dead look," as she and Leila referred to the slight glow about their skin. It was inherent to vampires, and it did appear otherworldly. That much he agreed with. But if she was going to cover the peppering of deep brown spots, he'd rather she glowed or whatever. Simply beautiful was the only descriptor that fit, and even that was too paltry a compliment. "I watched a bit of television some time ago and caught a few episodes of Xena," he said. "It was an interesting show. Amazons were never like that, exactly. Nor does Wonder Woman fit the bill, but I guess humans have lots of creativity in their lore. It's not like they have reliable reference tools."

"You knew Amazons?"

"Once."

"And did you date an Amazon?" He could feel her begin to scoot away from him, but he held tight.

"None of them hold a finger to you, Farrah."

"They'd better not. I know how to fight, in case you missed the memo."

"Yes, and if I run into an Amazon, I'll tell them to beware."

"No, only if you run into your ex."

"Okay, I'll keep that in mind."

Then she moved back into him, draping a leg over his and shifting up to rest her head on his shoulder after planting a quick kiss there.

Yes, he wanted to make love to her, but she was tired, and if he had to, he would let her rest. After all, he had so many lifetimes to please her. If he could help it.

CHAPTER SEVEN

Mael's recent decisions had been no less than problematic. Leila had refused to take no for an answer, and to keep the peace, he'd let her tag along with him. Which was how he'd ended up with the woman who seemed to get some kind of thrill out of torturing him. He shouldn't have allowed her to get under his skin. Or burrowed into his senses. He could still smell, taste, and feel her. She was on his mind, a priority in the middle of his shit show of a mess.

Since she'd come back into his life, there hadn't seemed to be any other way to live—with her crawling over his resolve. He'd said he would stop chasing Lily. Apparently, his plans and boundaries didn't matter at all when it came to her. Not in the slightest.

They watched their target from rooftops as he moved along through the winding city streets, the veil of night providing them cover along the way.

The distance between Melody and where they ended up was no more than two miles. Mael cursed under his breath. The building was not far from the warehouse where Leila and Farrah had been held captive a few weeks back, along with some other girls. It made sense that the bastards would operate in the vicinity, but Mael was frustrated that he and Anwar hadn't found them before now.

"You think this guy has something to do with the plot?" Leila whispered despite the loud traffic in the area. Some places in Detroit never quieted down, especially when that close to the interstate.

"It would make sense. One of the only things that seems to fit in this case. I want to get that building wired for sound. Think your boy can handle that?"

"Ennis? Yeah, I do. But why don't we just go in there and deal with him?"

Leila had always been the take-action type of female. He had to smile in her direction. "We could. But that won't help us if it's more than just him. We want to be sure we're getting all the players. One smooth hit."

Leila made some kind of chuckle combined with a snort. "Always been your way, hasn't it?"

"I was just thinking the same about you, love." Mael broke his gaze and returned it to the building across from the one they had perched on top of and whoever the guy was. He'd exited the vehicle once he'd parked and then went inside. There were no windows on the first level, so there was no way to tell what the man was doing in there. "We'll need eyes in there too."

"Yeah."

Mael could sense the note of apprehension in her voice as she leaned on the building's rooftop ledge. With a glance at the sky, he immediately understood. It was light-ening with the rising of the sun. "You need to get home.

It's around five. In another hour, you'll be in trouble out here exposed."

"Honestly," she said, voice lowered and deadly serious, "I know what I need to do to take care of myself."

"I hear you. But we didn't exactly drive here. In another minute or so, the world will be waking up. I don't want you to go viral because you were out here trying to finish something that's going to take weeks of surveillance... possibly."

Then she looked at him, finally. Probably for the first time since they'd damn near fucked earlier that evening. "I need to get this shit finished. I want our lives back. We don't have weeks, Mael."

"Okay, but did you hear me say possibly? Or are you just bound and determined to disagree with me on everything?"

"There isn't a thing I'm determined to do with you." Leila rolled her eyes skyward, taking in the dim glow on the horizon. "I'll get Ennis working on this when I get home. But if we have to sit on this bitch for the next few days, we will. Eire may not be as lucky as I was. I'm going to try to make sure she is safe, even if that means I have to be in lockstep with you every minute until she's home." Without another word, Leila started her smooth ascent into the heavens. She was an older vampire, so, although they didn't have wings, they had the ability to lift themselves into the air using sheer strength. One jump could carry them for miles. It was hella close to flight, and Leila made it look like an elegant dance.

"I'll text you the address," he screamed after her. It was perhaps one of the lamest replies, but it was the best he could come up with since his brain was scrambled just looking at her. Let alone having touched her and held her trembling legs locked in place over his neck. The first time in nearly a century. He licked his lips at the thought.

Thanks to the lug-head-ass bouncer down at her bar, he hadn't been able to service her properly. His cock twitched as he recalled her unfolding herself before him, her naked sex eager for his attention.

No matter if he hadn't been able to finish all the things he had in mind for her. Her decision to let him in had come swiftly, and he wasn't about to let the opportunity pass him by. For years, he'd thought of how she would feel, and as vivid as his memories of her were, he was so wrong. She was more confident, assured of what she wanted and how she wanted it to happen. Those characteristics turned him on more than he'd ever been before.

He watched her move through the sky until she became no more than a dot on the horizon. "Don't worry, Lily. I'll make it up to you." The words he spoke into the night sky were ones he would keep for the rest of his days. The vow enveloped his heart as he watched the sun creep over the horizon.

Though he hadn't wanted her to accompany him, her absence resonated in his body the moment her feet left the rooftop. She left him cold, the knowledge of how very alone he was more profound each time Leila, his Lily, ran away from him.

Reluctantly, he pulled his shit together and got the hell back online with the reason he was there. There were large windows on the upper floors of the dilapidated building, without glass in most. But the male seemed to have vanished.

In the early morning hours and in that particular neighborhood, there weren't many humans awake.

Leaping to the ledge, Mael unfurled his wings and flew across the expanse and in through an open window.

There was a combination of smells, from piss to mold to decaying vermin. He took in the room he'd landed in with a cautious eye. Using his sensory perception, he scanned for the telltale rhythmic pulsing and found none. He would have heard the slower beat of a human's heart or the rapid beating beneath a shifter's ribcage. Instead, there was nothing. Clearly, he'd missed the bastards again.

Mael stalked around the room on the second story and found a crumbling stairwell leading to the lower level of the warehouse. Instead of risking the whole thing collapsing beneath him, he omitted their use altogether and leaped to the floor beneath him. The smells were even worse downstairs, understandably. And the area over there was just as sparse as the upstairs had been.

There were a few broken tables and tattered blankets on a lopsided couch, evidence of the homeless staying there from time to time, most likely in an attempt to avoid the cold. He reached out again with his perception searching any sign of life, and there was nothing.

With one more scan of the building, he assumed the one he and Leila had been tracking had left somehow when he'd been distracted with her.

A wasted mission, though he didn't necessarily see it that way. Damn his foolish heart, but he had enjoyed the extra moments with her. If Mael got even another minute with his Lily, it was worth it.

CHAPTER EIGHT

The moment nightfall was upon her the following day, Farrah got dressed and ready to leave Anwar's. She had hoped their vigorous lovemaking would keep him sleeping. He had been curled around her like a comfortable, warm blanket when she'd untangled herself from his massive limbs and dressed in the rapidly darkening room. It was not her intention to be kept away from living her life. She could help look for Eire and keep her business going, despite what Anwar, and even Leila, believed about her. She wasn't some weakling who needed to be covered and protected all the time.

And while even she knew she had areas of improvement in the way of defending herself, there was no way shouldn't at least try. Anwar had been beside himself after last night's call and possible break-in, but she had been prepared, at least. Even if he hadn't walked her through the safe room procedures, she would have done it on her own, right?

She was almost home free, having scrawled a quick note explaining she was going to the VMA and heading for the door, shoes in hand.

"Where do you think you're going?"

Shit... Anwar wasn't exactly a contemporary man when it came to defending his female. He had made that clear and even told her on several occasions, but it was too hard for her to take the sit-back-and-do-nothing approach. "Actually, I just left you a note. I'm going to VMA, and Leila and I are going to discuss what happened last night."

His lips twisted as he stared at her. His big body was tense, concern creasing between his eyes. He was altogether spectacular and something akin to a caveman. "I don't think that's a good idea."

Turning to face him, she put her shoes on the floor to step into the blue and white Nike trainers. "I can see why you would be concerned, but if this guy is human, he probably isn't as strong as me—"

"We had this discussion already."

"We did, but I think I can help in some way."

"There is a male or... something stalking Leila's bar. We can assume he's after you. The only thing saving you has been that you haven't been at the VMA alone. This is a no-go, nonstarter, Farrah."

"Has anyone stopped to think Leila may be in danger too?" She leveled the coolest stare she could muster with him glowering like that. Even placed her hands on her hips for extra emphasis. There, in the middle of his austere penthouse with priceless paintings and the equivalent of a living museum, she was trying to outmaneuver an actual warrior prince—who happened to be her lover. What was life, even? Not too long ago, she had only dreamed of having a male to argue with in such a way. And while he was infuriating her at the moment, she still lost her breath looking at him.

"I'm coming with you, then. Give me a second and I'll get dressed."

"You can't come with me everywhere I go. It's not fair to you."

For some reason, her words seemed to trigger him. Anwar stalked over to her and stopped mere inches away.

Farrah needed to crane her neck to see him. When she found his eyes, he stared back at her with such ferocity she tightened inside. Not in a way that was domineering, but with such a deep pleading that she wanted to hold him. Of course, she couldn't because she was standing her ground.

"I will be wherever you need me. I don't care what it is, nothing is more important than you."

She let out a sigh and slowly nodded. "I guess, but you'll probably be very bored."

"With you? I highly doubt that."

"Okay, fine. Go get dressed."

"You should come with me. You can help me wash my back." Hooded eyes raked over her body, and immediately, she knew that wasn't all he wanted.

She should have been sore, or tired, or determined to find out what was going on, but something inside her wouldn't tell him no. The truth was, she was just as desperate to have him as he seemed to be to have her. "Okay, but then we're going straight to the VMA."

He made a cross over his naked chest, and gentle curves played at the corners of his lips. "Swear. Immediately after I'm dressed, we'll go straight there. We'll even drive. I can't expect you to sprint all over the city after what we're going to do." With that, he lifted her into his arms and carried her across the spacious living room, into the bedroom, then on to the bathroom where he sat her on the counter. "Don't go anywhere."

Making a cross over her own chest, she set her purse on the countertop and leaned back against the mirror. He was something to see, gorgeous in every way. She watched as he moved—the way his muscle worked in his back, the way his boxers gripped his ass. He turned on the water for a bath and tested the temperature before returning to her.

"You don't need this." He lifted her T-shirt, then ran strong hands over her waist and hips. "Nor these." He tugged at the leggings she'd slipped on that morning.

Farrah raised her lower body, allowing him to slip the pants from her. She was left in a bra and nothing else since she'd opted for commando. When all her clothes were on the floor, she leaned forward and nipped at his erect, deep brown bud. "Well, I'm here, so what are those things you promised to do to me?"

As her teeth grazed his nipple, something guttural came from his chest. The scent of him was heavenly, the spicy blend that somehow called to mind freshly fallen leaves. She could see from the front of his boxers he was aroused. The print of his cock strained against the fabric, and she wanted to take him all into her mouth. In fact, she was of a mind to do just that when he stopped her, his hands lifting her back up to eye level.

"Not yet," he growled. The capturing of her lips was quick, consuming as he invaded her.

Their bodies crashed against the mirror, the vibration of the impact running the length of its wall-to-wall surface. Farrah wrapped her legs around his waist, pulling him closer, the hunger taking control of her forcing her fangs to punch forward. Breaking the kiss, she sank them into his shoulder, biting down hard. Greedily, she drank down his life force, the taste a savory wine on her tongue. She gulped in, the fact that they hadn't negotiated who would feed lost in the eroticism of the moment.

A hand pressed her thigh open, the other going around her waist and pulling her to the front of the counter. His mouth was on her neck as he licked over the vein that seemed to pulse if only from his contact. "Drink from me," she whispered, only freeing her mouth from his body for a moment before taking another taste from a spot closer to his neck.

His body stilled, his cock barely penetrating her. She knew the implications, but he seemed to be unsure. It was only for a second, but in that time, her thoughts came back online.

Pulling away, she stopped her desperate lapping at him. Better to focus her attention anywhere other than on the most important thing in the room. In her life. "I mean, you could take me..." God, shit had gotten awkward quick, hadn't it? "You don't *have* to, though. I mean, I get it. It's a commitment."

The truth was, to drink from one another at the same time, they would be full-on blood-mated—she would be his and him, hers. It would mean that they would share strength and be dependent upon one another for more than just sex. It would be their hearts together as one. Their minds and souls connected until one of them died. A union.

"I know what it is. I just... I want to make sure you're ready for this. This is... well, relatively permanent. I'm just not a fan of making decisions in the heat of the moment."

"You mean, like when you're dick-deep inside me?" It was probably crass, but she needed the humor to ease some of her embarrassment.

Despite her joke, he didn't pull out. Instead, he pulled her a little closer, until he was inside her so deep, knowing where he stopped and she began was nearly impossible. Her body stretched around the familiar girth, accepting him. Welcoming him home. "I want you so goddamned much, Farrah. But this has to be something you're sure about. Whether you want to be with me forever. It's been a little over a month. But give yourself a few days. Think about it. This moment and all the others. If you still want to mate me after you've considered, I'm yours." Leaning down, he kissed her. It wasn't with the desperate lust of earlier. Instead, it was slow and intentional. The movement of his hips was deliberate as he pulled out then drove deep inside her with such a force, she trembled against him.

"Anwar..." she cried out, his name a strangled moan against his mouth.

He lifted her, both hands latched on to her ass. In an urgent move, Anwar's hand slipped over her flesh and searched desperately for the tight bud of her ass. A single finger slipped inside her, the resulting shiver nearly launching her over some imagined edge. She felt so full, so wanted, and so wet. Her muscles tightened around his cock, and it was as if fireworks went off inside her body. Blindingly vibrant and causing her to nearly seize.

Her nipples drew to taut points on her chest, and her first orgasm tore from her so hard, starbursts danced inside her shuttered lids. To catch her breath, she pulled away from his kiss, leaning back, her body arching over the strong arm wrapped tightly around her and holding her upright.

It was in that moment, as she came undone again and again, she knew she was already his. Mind. Body. Soul.

CHAPTER NINE

For the entire day, Leila thought about the feeling of Mael between her thighs. She'd chided herself, promised rewards for not thinking of him for a period of time, and fought hard against the furious masturbation session she'd ended up having. And then, she'd screamed his name when she'd reached her climax.

The main issue was she couldn't satisfy herself the way she needed. There was only one male who would be able to do that. She promised herself she would not allow him to take her again. She would not dare to tempt fate again.

It was two hours after nightfall, and she was still waiting on Farrah to arrive at the VMA so she could tell her about their wild chase across the city. She would, of course, omit her moment of weakness with Mael... most likely. She hated keeping things from her progeny and, even more, felt as if she had harshly judged Farrah for her involvement with someone affiliated with the Order. Wasn't Mael the same? There was actually no difference at all. So now to admit to the same weakness made her feel... well, pathetic.

She was about to head over to Melody when Farrah came in looking happy and sated. Leila knew the look because she'd had the same long ago... whenever she and Mael had spent the day making love.

No, not love-making. They had been just having sex. Mael couldn't have walked away from her if he'd truly felt the same as she had.

"Well, it's about time. I won't bother asking where you've been. And don't worry. I don't have a thing to do except wait for you," she said. Was the ice on the end of her words from being annoyed at waiting for a couple hours, or was it jealousy? She knew, she thought, the answer but wasn't quite ready to face it. Farrah had been blessed with something Leila knew wasn't in the cards for her. Every male she'd had after Mael had been a pale imitation of him. Someone to take a romp with in the hay. The truth was, Mael was the exact reason she hated the notion of mating. It was because, despite being as close as she'd ever been to a male, he'd still walked out on her.

"I'm sorry. Anwar is a little bit overprotective right now. It took me a while to convince him to go on about his night and that he didn't need to come here. He's having a hard time trusting Ennis's security system. How'd you and Mael get on last night?" Farrah latched the door behind herself using her will and continued walking over until she reached the counter and dropped her purse off.

Leila got up from her favorite sofa in the pretend antique furniture store. To humans, it was the Vintage Modernism Authority. Only a select clientele knew what it really was—the Vampire Matchmaking Agency. Along the way, she made sure to roll her eyes skyward, though she understood the reasons Farrah couldn't resist Anwar. "I think you may need to consider some bodyguards. Not that I want to agree with your boo, but it is getting dangerous."

"I know that. But it feels like I'm allowing someone to stop me from living my life and doing the things that I know are helping people." She tapped a few times on the computer to awaken it, not even bothering to look up as Leila made it across the room.

"I think you know there has to be some self-preservation considered, otherwise you won't be able to help anyone. You get that, right?"

"Of course I do." Deep brown eyes rose to meet Leila's. She was showing concern, which was the right reaction.

Leila wondered if Farrah truly understood what that meant. That putting others' needs before her own was to endanger herself. And if whoever was targeting them was somehow getting information on Farrah's clients and acting on it, which seemed to be the way things were working out, Farrah was endangering her clients as well. Leila just needed to get her willful friend to see that.

"Girl, we need to slow this thing down. I do think you should live your life. But you are going to have to care about the potential consequences. Anwar can't be around to shield you all the time."

"I never asked him to do that. Never. This isn't the way I wanted things to turn out, either. We still can't find Eire. It's almost all I can think about. So I need to hang on to some normalcy. By my fingernails, if I have to." Farrah slammed the laptop closed with such force Leila was sure the screen was destroyed.

"Listen, I get that. We've all made some... strange

decisions since this whole thing began. I know that firsthand."

Farrah quirked a brow in her direction.

That was right, she didn't know about Leila's momentary indiscretion or all the wild fantasies starring Mael. "But the point is, you can't just walk around blind to the fact that others are at risk. Speaking of, did Mael tell you what happened last night?"

"No... what's up?"

"Anwar didn't say anything, either?" Leila was surprised. Then again, maybe not. Mael hadn't wanted her going along, and she could totally see them hiding something like that from Farrah. When Farrah shook her head, Leila continued. "That guy they saw on the traffic cam? He showed up at the club again. Same car and everything."

This pulled Farrah out of doom-and-gloom land if her reaction was any clue. She leaned forward, one hand gripping the countertop. "And?"

"And nothing. It was too risky to barge into the building without knowing whether or not there was a trap waiting for us. Mael and Anwar are going back over there. At least, that's what Mael said. We're going to have to wait and take our cues from them."

Farrah pondered for a little while, a pensive and worried look tightening her features. "So, did Anwar know about it?"

"I don't know that for sure. When I left Mael on the rooftop across from where we think they could be hiding out, he hadn't told him. And since you just left him, I'm guessing he just hasn't had a chance to call Anwar. I'm sure they'll want a second to investigate."

"And what do you think?"

"Honestly, I think there could be things that are outside of our league. Mael is a fallen with some good fighting skills, and I'm pretty sure Anwar was trained for just such an occasion. We may do more harm than good by going there. I don't think Anwar is able to concentrate when you're around. It's adding an extra layer for something to go down."

"Well, I know how to stay out of the way."

"Girl, you cannot be serious. It's not a good idea. You asked how I felt, and now that I've given it, you won't accept it."

Farrah let out a sigh before walking away from the counter and heading to a Barcalounger, flopping into it, and bringing her feet upright as she lay there contemplating the alternative to what Leila had just imparted. "So, I'm just supposed to sit here with my thumb up my butt?"

"I'm going to tell you again, none of this is possible if you're harmed. The VMA will fold, and all the clients will be left with nowhere to turn. Is that what you want?"

"No. Of course, I don't. I just want to be useful."

"Yeah, well. You can be useful by letting Anwar focus on the task at hand. Not to mention the Order could bring charges before you since they all know about VMA. We have to deal with what they could do to us, and we should probably be very careful about who we allow around us. Eire was a... *is* a fae, and if she were with the Order, she could have taken back some serious intel. Use your head, my friend. We have too much going on to splinter your attention."

This statement made Farrah's eyes clamp down tight. Perhaps she hadn't heard her, maybe tuned out the "momming," as she liked to call it.

"Fine." It was all Farrah said for the next few moments.

Leila felt the urge to spill all the beans from somewhere deep inside herself. It was a joke, honestly. She wasn't the type to hold back anything. And it was what she prided herself most on. "There's something else too," she stated. She didn't know where to begin, but it couldn't be something she never shared. "I'm going to ask you for no judgment on this one, though."

"You slept with Mael." Farrah's tone was matter-of-fact and razor-sharp against Leila's chest plate.

"How did you know that?"

"Easy," she said, sitting up with a smirk. "You smell just like him still." Farrah tapped the side of her nose. "And you would smell it too if you weren't used to it. I think it's probably safe to fling that closet door open... especially since it's made of glass." She waited for the footrest to fold neatly into the chair and leveled a glance at Leila.

"First of all, I didn't exactly sleep with him..."

"Ohhhh. So, what did you do?" Serious Farrah was gone, leaving behind the fourteen-year-old-girl version.

"It's not like that. We were in the middle of an argument, and next thing you know, his wings stood at attention and his head was between my thighs. I might still be there if one of the bouncers hadn't come to the door. That's when we went after the guy."

"Leila, if you want Mael, that's perfectly fine. You're allowed to date males at your leisure."

"Yeah, but I'm not allowed to date *him*. He hasn't done anything to show me he's not a lying asshole. Giving me amazing oral on my desk does nothing to reassure me."

"Remind me never to eat at your desk again."

"Funny," Leila snapped, allowing her body to practically collapse onto the deep blue couch directly across from Farrah.

Farrah chuckled and tossed her a side-eye that clued Leila in she wasn't buying her shit. "So, better than you remembered? Because I'm pretty sure you've already completed an in-depth analysis of whether or not his skills improved."

"We didn't do anything except a few minutes of heavy petting."

"That's not an answer to my question."

"It was quick and just so dirty. I don't want to think about it. It makes my stomach a little queasy."

"Okay, but I think you know and just don't want to admit it to yourself." Farrah was full-on smiling at that point.

"Fine. He has a very good mouthpiece on him. You happy now?" Taking a throw pillow from the spot next to her, Leila smashed it over her face to hide her embarrassment.

"I don't think I know this Leila. 'Cause you're pretty open about your sexuality. And if I didn't know better, I'd think you're uncomfortable because last night meant more to you than you're letting on."

This statement, more than any other, set Leila's blood on fire. How dare she come for her like that? "Girl, all Mael is to me is a way to blow off some steam. It's all he'll ever be to me. That's it." She was practically yelling at her friend, her voice louder and more forceful. In fact, the only thing that stopped her from going on, vehemently explaining her position, was the wide-eyed, blank stare right past her to something immediately behind her.

She didn't want to look because the back of her neck

was hot. She already knew what she would find but couldn't stop herself from checking with a quick glance back.

Tossing an arm over the couch, she slowly, regretfully turned to find Mael and Anwar, standing near the front door.

"I um... I thought I'd use my key," Anwar started, before casting a glance at Mael, whose eyes were downcast.

Damn their timing. The last thing Leila wanted was for him to know she cared enough to talk about him. How she felt, what she thought of him, was none of his business. He didn't need to know whether he rated with her at all. And judging from the look on his face, he knew more than he should.

Fuck my life...

CHAPTER TEN

ANWAR

Never one to feel secondhand embarrassment for anyone, Anwar sure felt it then. The heat coming off Mael was palpable, and one glance at Leila told him she hadn't wanted him to hear her last statement. This wasn't rocket science. Something had gone down between them, and Mael had apparently been on the receiving end of the Mack truck Leila was driving.

"So, um... I used my key. Sorry. Should have announced before just coming on in." Anwar ran a hand along the back of his neck, fingers tangling in the locs pinned low at his nape.

"Oh, sure. Yeah, that's fine. We were just talking about... uh... one of my clients."

Anwar made a note to himself to never ask Farrah to lie about anything because she was terrible—not only did her explanation sound terrible, but she also had a terrible poker face, the bluffing evident in her wide eyes and uncomfortable smile. Back in his day, they would play around the mouths of volcanoes and get scolded by their mothers. He'd seen some of his cousins with that exact same look.

"It's cool, Farrah. Some of us are comfortable with our uses," Mael said, pinning Leila with a scathing glance, then breaking the connection with a shake of his head.

The male stalked his bulky body past Anwar and headed for the desk in the center of the room. He leaned on it, then took his phone out of his pocket and started scrolling. With the tense atmosphere in the room, Anwar wished they would just screw already. Granted, Mael probably wished the same. It had been over a month of them at one another's throats, and Anwar started to wonder if they didn't secretly enjoy the battles.

"Any word from Ennis on the caller?" Anwar walked over to sit next to his girl. There wasn't any time that he didn't want to crawl all over Farrah. She was the female who set his world on its axis.

"No," she said, placing a quick—too quick—peck on his lips. "But it's harder to trace cells, and we can't omit that it might have been a burner. Perhaps he's able to pick up the general vicinity of where the call came from, but it would be far from exact. What about the guy Leila and Mael traced yesterday? We were just getting to that. Any more on him?" She glanced at the two of them, and both were looking anywhere except at one another.

"I stopped by the warehouse earlier tonight. There was nothing. I didn't break in since I wasn't sure whether there was an ambush, but I did sit on it. No one in or out. And the Order is getting us the traffic cam videos from last night through this afternoon. We may be able to see if he went back there at any point, but from what I could tell, the warehouse was largely empty." Mael rattled all that off in the same monotone voice he'd used since they'd come in.

"Can't you just go in there and see what's going on?" Farrah shifted in her seat to face Mael. She seemed concerned, her brows furrowed as she asked the question, and Anwar could tell she was getting more and more anxious to resolve the situation.

Anwar placed a hand over hers, webbing their fingers together in the hopes of calming her down a bit. She had been a wreck since he'd gotten her back from the kidnappers, which was completely understandable. It would take more than a few weeks to get over something like that. "No, it's best to hang back for a minute. We need to be sure we get them all, otherwise, they'll just keep on coming back for whatever it is they want."

"It just doesn't seem right. There haven't been human hunters for years in these parts. What could be so important that they would stalk us?" Though she'd asked the question, Leila hadn't looked up from picking at her cuticles.

"I don't know, but eventually, like no-good fuckers are prone to do, they'll show their hand," Mael answered.

"I wasn't talking to you, Mael."

"Cool, cool... must not need to be serviced, then, right?"

Those were the words that brought both their heads up, eyes locked in a battle of wills. Clearly, she was not there for his shit, even if she'd kind of started them off with what Mael had overheard. And he was not going to take her abuse lying down anymore. Whatever it was, both Anwar and Farrah were squirming a bit, considering it was their two best friends going to war. Anwar wasn't sure which way was better, but he knew they shouldn't be privy to whatever was about to go down. "Hey, babe. Did you bring your servers back online for VMA? If so, can we work back at my place?"

Both Anwar and Farrah also knew if they went back to his penthouse at Westborn Towers, there was no way they were working. It was the exact reason she always wanted to go to the agency to get things done. It was something she would probably get used to one day—at least Anwar hoped. Since they were so new and fresh, though, it wasn't like he could stop himself. He adored touching her. Even if that wasn't the reason he wanted to rush her out of there that evening, it was definitely a benefit. Bringing her knuckles to his mouth, he kissed them. She'd just left him, and he was already preoccupied with the feel of her body beneath his.

"I actually did. I have a few clients. Particularly Mr. Batchelor. I was supposed to hook him up with Eire, and... well, then everything happened. He probably thinks there's no hope." Her eyes normally lit from within when he touched her. In that moment, she seemed nearly unreachable.

"I promise, I'll let you work to find him a suitable match. I won't distract you at all."

Farrah smirked. "That's what you say now. And who says it'll be you doing the distracting? All right, I'll grab my laptop. And we can check in with Ennis on the way. Maybe he has something." As she stood, she glanced over at her maker. "So, you going to Melody or staying here?"

Anwar could feel the heat rise a degree in the room. One thing about the fallen, they were definitely capable of changing the barometer if they felt things strongly enough. Their moods could affect the very air around

them. Anwar had never seen him behave that way over a woman, though. And while they hadn't spent time discussing what Mael felt for Leila, Anwar knew it was no ordinary feelings or a passing fling. And he hoped his friend could salvage whatever love they'd shared once upon a time.

"No, I think I'm going to check some of my other clubs tonight. Hence, I won't need the chaperone." She sent another positively frigid glare in Mael's direction. "So, I'll lock up for you."

"Okay, but do you think it's cool for you to stay here by yourself?" Farrah's look of concern was back again. These days, it was never too far away.

Anwar honestly didn't want her to press the issue. Maybe Mael would stay behind too, and they could work out whatever shit was going on between them. It was even on the tip of his tongue, but he knew better than to get in between matters of the heart. When the chips fell, he would be there to listen, to have a shot of whiskey with the poor bastard if needed, or if they were to end up somewhere in the realm of happily ever after, he'd dance at their mating. Until then, he would shut the fuck up and pray for the best.

"I'm a big girl, Farrah. You go ahead with Anwar. I'd feel better if you were somewhere they didn't know about and with obstacles to get to you."

"Fine. Just make sure you reset the alarm when you're leaving. Ennis updated the system to include a laser or some such shit. He really got off on it. I told him he may need to let me hook him up with someone."

"Yeah, well, he's not the only one," Mael said.

Anwar, who'd been standing up, shifted his eyes in his friend's direction. "Bro, you coming with us? I can drop you somewhere." He was trying to throw him a lifeline, but he could already see from Mael's face that he wasn't going to bite.

"Nah. I'll make sure your girl gets out, then I'm heading home."

Home? While Anwar knew Mael had somewhere he went occasionally, he mostly spent his nights in the other wing of Anwar's penthouse. It was the length of half a city block, after all, and most of the time, he and Mael never saw one another unless it was intentional. "You know I'm not putting you out, right?" He had to be sure that Mael knew he was welcome, even when Farrah was there.

"I do. I'm good, though. I'll come by before sunset tomorrow. And I'll put that warehouse, as well as the building nearby, under surveillance. Maybe our friend will show up again with whoever he's working for. He doesn't look bright enough to be more than a low-level burglar. I just have a feeling."

On second thought, Anwar almost wanted to drag him out of there. Mael could be pretty stubborn and wasn't the best at taking no for an answer. He was an archangel, and they were more about claiming than consent, despite it being the twenty-first century. From what he could tell, Mael was on a short leash as far as Leila was concerned and one step from crawling around behind her on all fours. But he didn't want his desperation to get the better of him. "Ah, can I talk to you for a second... outside?" Better safe than sorry.

Mael only nodded before peeling his big body up from the desk and stomping out the door.

"Okay. So, I'll meet you outside, then," Farrah said.

"Yeah, I just need to"—he glanced over at Leila, who

was still sitting ramrod straight on the funky blue couch that had to be from the sixties—"you know, make sure his head is on straight. I don't want to have to come back here and scrape him off the ceiling if shit goes left." He tried to say it low, but the super-strong hearing of Atlanteans was another trait they'd passed on to their evolutionary byproducts.

"I think that's a great idea," Farrah said. "I'll give y'all a couple of minutes before coming out."

"Yeah, we don't need too long." Anwar pulled the keys to his '67 Impala from his pocket. It was his new favorite since his Charger had been blown to bits in the Tabernacle parking lot last month. Yet another reason he wanted to get the bastards responsible. As if trying to harm Farrah hadn't been enough. "I'll see you around, Leila."

She didn't lift her head but did give him a cursory nod. While that was in no way exactly a jovial reply, he would take it. There was a time when she wouldn't have said a damned thing to him. She still didn't trust his involvement with the Order. As she shouldn't. The Order was going to be hard-pressed to do something to VMA since it was the worst-kept secret across the supernatural diaspora.

He didn't press his luck with Leila, though. Instead, he headed for the front door and blew Farrah a kiss over his shoulder as he stepped out into the muggy night air. "Aye, man. You sure you need to stay here? Leila looks like she could tear you apart, and I honestly don't know which of you I trust the least around one another. I don't want either of you hurt, but without Leila, Farrah would be a mess. And I need to make sure she's always good, you got me?"

"I do. But trust me, I need to get some things off my chest. It's not going to get any better if I let it fester. This conversation is seventy-five years overdue." The shrug was probably meant to portray mild interest, that Mael was good no matter what went down. But it hadn't worked.

Mael had clearly forgotten that Anwar knew most everything about him. He was normally light-spirited, but not about things he cared about. So, while it was a good playoff, Anwar knew the brother was being ripped apart inside. You could never truly fool a friend. "You don't think you need to cool off a bit?"

It was then another veil of hurt slipped over his friend's features. His face twisted, mouth agape before the calm mask fell back into place. "I would never... I would not dare to harm Leila. Nor any female. If that's what you're insinuating, you, Anwar, can fuck right off."

"I didn't mean it like that. I just don't want you two in there doing something to one another you'll regret. It's more than just sex. She could literally hurt you. And if, all things being equal, you could—"

"Let her beat the shit out of me if she wants. You're right, that might happen. Hell, it wouldn't be anything new. If you recall, the first time I walked into Melody, she threw a highball glass at my head. I was picking glass shards out of my neck for at least twenty-four hours. She's got a helluva right hook. And if she uses it, it wouldn't be because I don't deserve it. Now, go get your female, and I'll see you tomorrow."

Anwar hesitated a minute because what else could he say? It wasn't as if he didn't know the feeling. If Farrah one day decided to jack him in his sleep, the only thing he would do would be to try to hold her down. That was all he had. The idea of her being so angry that she'd hit him was upsetting on its own. But down to his marrow, he would react in just the way Mael described. "All right. I'll see you, then. And Mael, if you find that bastard, you call me. Let's get this shit handled, yeah?"

"Yeah," Mael said, holding out his hand to dab him, and Anwar returned the same.

As if on cue, Farrah came outside, the scents of vanilla and lilac accompanying her and making Anwar glad he was taking her home. "Ready, guys?"

"I am." Anwar smiled down at her as she stepped into the crook of his arm. "And Mael, you two need to talk it out, you know?"

"I do. Have a good night. I'll call you if I turn something up."

"Bet. Tomorrow."

Anwar walked Farrah over to his car and got her settled in the passenger seat before heading around to his own door. He glanced back up at Mael, who hadn't moved a muscle. He stood outside VMA. The day shields were up, and through the window, he could see Leila sitting on the couch, head laid back into the cushions and with the exact same forlorn look as her would-be man.

Yeah, Anwar hoped they worked it out. If they couldn't be lovers, perhaps they would be friends. Because if they didn't, one of them would have to go to spare Farrah the stress. After all, Mael wasn't the only one who would do anything for the female he loved.

CHAPTER ELEVEN

The door made some noise upon Mael's entry. Leila knew it was him from his scent and his aura. That was the one thing about him. He would never be able to sneak up on her because, unlike Anwar and Farrah, Mael and Leila had exchanged blood in what seemed now to be eons ago. It was different when non-vampires exchanged blood with vampires, though. It left the same type of echo in the blood, the same feelings of loss when apart, and unfortunately, if one of them were to die, the other would know nearly instantly. However, they did not share their strength, and unlike vampires, they could mate again with someone else.

She'd prayed, in the depths of her pain many years ago, that she would finally be free either through her own death or his. The relief in the early years would have been a sweet victory, of sorts. The freedom to be her own person again. She'd never shared that she had exchanged blood with him, but her experience with Mael, and his ultimate betrayal, was the source of her knowledge on matters of the heart. He'd taught her the hard way that love didn't pay.

She stood from her seat after the silence stretched for too many beats. "You want to yell at me about what I said, Mael?" She wasn't in much of a mood to mince words. If they were going to get into it, might as well get it on.

"Nope. I want to understand what that was last night." His eyes were liquid blue, and she'd never seen them that way unless they were doing other things.

"That was fucking. Or almost fucking. I would think I wouldn't have to tell you that."

A sardonic laugh escaped him as he took a step closer and shoved his hands in the pockets of the elegant black suit. "Oh no, that's not what that was. Trust me, I know the difference when it comes to you. What that was, was you taking the opportunity to punish me. Simply because you could. But what I don't know was why."

"Mael, we should have talked about this last night. Now, it feels... what's the word I'm searching for? Reductive." She had to break away from his stare. It was filled with ice and vitriol. It was nothing like the look he used to give her. This hurt male was just a shell of who he used to be. And she'd known, between her words and actions the night before, she'd done that to him. Surprisingly. Regretfully.

"Call it what you want, but you used me."

"And you haven't used me before?" Leila was walking away, trying to put some distance between them. Every bit of the ache he felt in his heart was alive underneath her flesh. She could feel it inside her just as she could feel air in her lungs and a knife in the gut.

Before she could make it to the refuge of the counter

to serve as a physical barrier between him and his pain, he was in front of her.

With strong arms, he grabbed her shoulders and stared at her, the intensity nearly overwhelming. "I never used you, Leila. I would have never. You couldn't understand the things I was going through then, and I'm not asking you to now, but I am asking—I'm begging you—to stop doing what you're doing."

She could feel the tears welling in the corners of her eyes, but through sheer will, she blinked them away. "Let go of me," she said, struggling out of his grip. "I'm not doing anything to you. I don't know what you expect. Did you think you would walk in here, say a few pretty words, and everything would be okay?"

"I expected you to hear me out, and if we couldn't do anything else, I wanted us to at least be civil."

"You killed civility years ago, Mael. After claiming you loved me, that you would do anything for me, you walked out. It wasn't something you even gave me a chance to warm up to. Just left. What was it you said?" A wild spurt of laughter escaped from her. "You said your brother needed you. In the span of ten minutes, you were gone. You didn't beg my forgiveness then. And you certainly didn't come back to try and fix what you broke."

"I couldn't. It was too dangerous. Someone would have found out what you meant to me and used it against me. I couldn't risk it. And then, when I... when I fell, I still had an obligation to Azazel. It's not something I could share. I didn't want to lie to you. I would never lie to you. So, I stayed away. Until... until now. I promise you, I had no idea you were involved with the VMA, nor that you were Farrah's maker. I was just trying to help Anwar."

"Well... here we are. You didn't know, but here you

stand. In my face, in my life. You think I need to be back there, the stupid one who believed that someone else could fill a space in my heart? You think I want to be reminded of the sad girl I once was?"

"Dammit... your heart is the best part of you. And I will have to live the rest of eternity knowing that I damaged the most beautiful thing, the most precious heart I've known in all these millennia. I don't need to be reminded of my mistakes, nor that you hate me. I carry the pain with me every day. And shall forevermore."

Oh, fuck you. "Fuck you, Mael," she spat out. Her chest heaved with anger like she'd run a mile back when she was human. It wasn't fair that he got to walk back into her life and penetrate the armored cage she'd constructed around her heart. There was no way she could possibly get the raggedy thing back in place when he walked away again.

"I deserve it, Leila. All the things you need to say and do to me. But I don't know if I can take it. Last night, I was ready. I would have taken a dagger and pierced my own heart if you had uttered the request. But I can't be both. You can't hate me and then take me to your bed because... because my heart can't take it. So, what's it going to be? Do you hate me, or do you want me as your lapdog? I simply don't have the capacity for both." Mael had been holding his hands out to her as if in surrender. He suddenly allowed them to drop to his sides. With a step backward, he leaned against the desk, and in another moment, he slid to the floor.

He was listless, the fiery glow in his eyes dying down to a muted overcast-sky tone, and it was as if the strength had drained right out of him and spilled into a dank pool around his body.

And had he been right? Had she simply toyed with him because she had the opportunity? The truth was, as much as she'd felt like she'd had the upper hand, that too was a fallacy. She remembered the way his skin felt against her inner thigh, felt the echoes of his pulse as she took blood from his femoral artery, and her pussy ached with need as the distant memory of him inside her flared back to life.

And now, with him practically on his knees, she didn't want to abuse him anymore. The little experiment with taking back her power from the one who hurt her the most had failed. If anything, she had turned what little strength she had over to him completely. With everything that she'd worked so hard to build up against him stripped from her, there was nothing left to do. With him before her, she knew it was useless to try to make him pay. Perhaps he'd been paying right alongside her.

Lowering herself, she sat on the floor in front of him, legs splayed out and ensuring no part of her body touched his. She wasn't ready for that again, not just yet. There was no way she would be able to withstand anything physical with Mael if they were just going to be civil. In truth, she was not going to stop being around Farrah, and Mael and Anwar seemed to be a package deal. Maybe she would see him less after they put a stop to whatever was going on around them with the humans, but there would always be moments their lives would intertwine. When they would have to see one another. They would probably always be in the same city, the same time. And she would always feel him until one of them was no more.

Yeah. He had been right. But there was no sense in telling him that. "So, what do we do now?" Leaning back on her hands, she crossed her legs and stared at the tips of her heels, the pointy shape enough of a distraction to keep her attention away from the mess she'd made with one selfish action.

"I don't know... maybe we could catch up? It's been a long time since I've seen you."

"Pssh. I don't think I want to know about how many women you've slept with, so if we must trek down memory lane, you can spare me those details."

"Oh, good. That's easy, and I can relieve your burden. None. I haven't been with anyone after you. It kind of seemed pointless, you know. They would never measure up to you, anyway. And I could... I can still feel you." He rubbed at his chest, then laid the hand on his lap.

"Now you must think I'm Booboo the Fool. You don't have to lie, Mael. Everyone has needs."

"And those needs come with some emotional baggage I wasn't ready to take on. So I pushed you, and the idea of sex, to the back of my mind. It's not that bad once you get used to it."

"You're kidding, right?"

"No... and for so many nights, I wished I was able to let it go. But nothing ever worked. It all led back to you."

"I'm not sure I believe you, but it's a nice sentiment. Thank you."

"You're welcome. And you know, it's no big deal. It's easy to talk to you. Though it's been years, it still hasn't worn off—our blood mating. Not for me anyway. I have to tell you the truth. Beyond that, I... Leila, I just *want* to tell you the truth. It's a relief."

While this caused her to pause, she didn't press the matter. "I'm glad you feel like you can be honest with me."

"Not just honest, open with you. That's so much more important."

"I guess I can see that."

"But you know what I wanted to ask you?"

"What?" she said, sure he couldn't throw her for a loop given he'd just bared his soul. And, for some reason, though she shouldn't, she believed him.

"What happened to the necklace?"

For a moment, Leila froze. She of course remembered the topaz-and-diamond pendant on a gorgeous eighteen-carat gold necklace. But she'd wanted to toss it away, hadn't she? Just like she'd thrown his clothes in a trash compactor. Discarded them so that she wouldn't have any more reminders to open the wounds in her heart. "I'm not sure. It's been a long time, Mael."

"I see. I was hoping... but I understand. I know how badly I hurt you." A faint smile that didn't quite reach his eyes traveled across his full lower lip.

The discomfort in the pit of her stomach as a result of her lie was worth it to afford herself at least a little protection. She was so afraid of giving herself over to him again. Somehow, no matter what she did, this internal battle she fought to maintain her distance from Mael was taking its toll.

In that moment, sitting on the floor with him and not hating him so much, she felt another bit of the armor fall away from her heart. Fortunately for her, she still had plenty to keep her out of his arms. For good.

At least, that's what she was banking on.

CHAPTER TWELVE

*Y*ears had passed since Mael had dared to dream of her. Not like the sex parts, but this—stripped down to nothing emotionally and nothing to keep them from baring their souls to one another.

She'd obviously forgotten that one of his abilities was sight—which meant it was pretty hard to deceive him. Even without it, he knew all of her tells. Whatever she'd done with it, she had reservations. Considering their past, Mael couldn't exactly blame her.

"I guess things have really changed over the last few years, haven't they? You aren't so vulnerable anymore."

"And you aren't all 'I'm an angel of the highest order' anymore, either, right? Back in the day, you were all about smiting and duty."

Mael let his head fall against the marble desk. "Well, rock bottom comes up fast. I gave up everything for my loyalty to Heaven, you know? And then, because I was trying to save my brother, the thing we'd been trained to do, I was shut out. It was a hard fall. But that's how it goes up there." He'd gotten used to saying *up* when in actuality, Heaven was more adjacent than up.

Leila stretched out on the floor like she was getting comfortable, and he had to admit, it was a nice sight to see her offering up her vulnerable side to him. Silky purple strands spilled over her elegant fingers. "Regrets? You ever feel bad about the things you did or didn't do?"

"Man, I think if I had to do it all again"—Mael brushed at invisible lint on his black slacks—"I wouldn't change a thing." He would, though, wouldn't he? "Except for you. You, I would walk through Hell barefoot to get you back. I wish I was joking," he said, the following chortle coming out a little less masculine than he wanted.

In reply, Leila's perfect lips twisted on the ends, and she rolled her eyes. Which, from her, meant she didn't hate him at the moment. And that was a blessing.

"What about you? What have you been up to since the twentieth century?"

"Damn, you know how to make a girl feel young. I'll ignore that age thing since—" She gestured to the general vicinity, insinuating everything. "Not much. Got myself a progeny, stopped partying all over the globe in exchange for a few bars and apartment buildings. I guess that's the normal track for becoming a mom, right?"

"Yeah, as much as I became a dad. Guess we're par for the course." Well, shit. In all the years he'd known Anwar and Constantine, he'd never once slipped up on Lani. Less than twenty-four hours after having his mouth on Leila's pussy, he'd confessed to his deepest secret.

"How's that? I mean, I know Anwar can be a bit of a brooder, but he's nothing like a newborn vampire," she said, the lilt of amusement in her voice.

For the first time in the whole conversation, he did

want to withhold something from her. If anything were to happen, she couldn't be implicated by knowing about it. Angels could be merciless when administering punishment. "Yeah... well, there was a reason I left to defend Azazel."

It didn't take long for all the amusement to leave Leila as she monitored him. "What do you mean?" She knew, though. Mael could sense her putting the pieces together.

"I wasn't just going to deal with yet another senseless war for Azazel. He had made an error. One that was supposed to cause everyone he'd ever touched pain."

Her eyes slitted and she studied him. "I'm not sure I understand."

Mael sucked in air and blew it out, the sound akin to defeat. "He slipped, Leila. With a human. And I knew of it. His mistake. His child."

A chill went up her spine. Everything she'd ever heard about Nephilim, and the reason they had been exterminated in ancient times, flooded back into her mind. They were dangerous. Categorically so. "There's no such thing as Nephilim, Mael."

Mael shook his head. "No, there weren't any before she was born. And Azazel and his human lover were supposed to be buried along with that infant."

"I-I hope you aren't saying what I think you're saying—"

"When the higher-ups in Heaven found out about her, orders were sent to all the archangels. We were to round them up. Murder the three of them. Burn their bones and bury them around the globe."

"But Azazael was your friend. How could you do that?"

"I did what I had to do. Before we received our orders,

though, he called to me. And I went. It was then he asked me to do something that would forever alter my destiny." He looked to her, hoping she would stop him so he wouldn't have to say the words out loud. It was something he'd never planned to do, but somehow, with her, he needed to lay the burden down. When she didn't say anything, he continued. "I killed him. I murdered him and his human woman. Because he asked me to." The tears slipped from him as easily as the blood had spilled after slitting their throats.

"Hang on one second. I'm just going to... I'll be right back," she said, rising to her feet with her brows knit in worry.

When she disappeared to somewhere behind him, he punched at the tears on his cheeks and rubbed his hands on his pants, trying to erase all evidence of his pain. His sin.

She was back with a bottle of Uncle Nearest and two shot glasses. "Thankfully, Farrah isn't much of a drinker, so this is here. I feel like we need it," she said, coming down with legs folded in front of her. This time, she was closer, and he could smell her citrusy perfume, refreshing to his senses. She poured two shots and held one out to him, her face still a mask, her mouth pressed into a thin line. "Drink, Mael."

He took it, and the smooth warmth burned its way to his chest after he turned the glass up to his lips. "I couldn't bring myself to do what he asked. To cut the babe from its mother... He wanted me to... I just couldn't."

"Then what did you do?" she said, taking her own shot.

There wasn't judgment in her eyes, not yet. He knew though, the next part of the story, the thing he'd omitted, was probably going to drive a nail into his coffin with her. It felt too good, though, to unburden himself after so many years. "When I cut them down, the knife was already bloody because he'd taken the baby from the womb... He cut..." No more words would come, and while he should have hanged his head in shame for what he and Azazel had done, he locked eyes with his Lily. He needed to see if she was going to send him away forever and their momentary reprieve where she pretended to give a damn about him would be over.

Pouring more drinks, she shook her head. The brown liquid filled the glasses and then sloshed over the sides as she handed him one then took her own, fast. When she was done, she swallowed deeply. "And the babe?"

"I took her to a hospital. She passes for human, and once every fifty years, she starts her life over again. It's my penance, you know? To her family, it seems as if she dies young. But I know. And I dig her up, then take her back to a hospital. She's been through a cycle already. Her name is Lelania, and in her previous life, she left a devastated fiancé and a daughter named Mallory. I watch over her too. Mallory is thirty right now, older than her mother is. Leilani is a twenty-six-year-old street vendor this time, and she is making a mess of this round." He drank down the whiskey once more.

"Why the cycles?"

"It's a curse. If she were among angels, she would draw on their strength and live a life similar to ours. Immortal. But she doesn't know. No one does. It seems I've managed to hide her very well. It's been my job since Azazel was felled. I made him a vow, and I'm still honoring it." Mael held the shot glass out to his Lily. If she hadn't thrown him out by now, he may as well finish the goddamned story.

"Well, what are you going to do about it? Just live your life as some kind of grim reaper, and she never finds out who she really is?"

"It's necessary." When she handed him another full shot glass, he had to smile. "You're a pretty good bartender, you know that?"

"So I've been told," she said, followed by a chortle.

"But there is someone who knows. And she's made me do some terrible things... to Anwar."

"Do I want to know?" This time, instead of tossing the drink back, she took a sip and set the glass down with half the contents remaining.

"Baby, did you want to know any of this shit?"

"Probably not, no," she said.

Damn, she was beautiful. Beyond her appearance, she accepted him, even after he'd shared some of the vilest parts of his existence. Some of the most horrible things he'd done to and for those he'd cared for. "It's Viktoria. She found out somehow, and, wouldn't you know, she exploited the knowledge. She made me take Anwar to VMA so he would violate the rules of the accords. The Order would never allow him to mate outside of his own kind unless it was a bride of their choosing. If he were to break this accord, the Atlanteans will be thrown out of the Order. Then, the Vampires wouldn't have any barriers to being the highest-ranking faction. Membership comes with privileges, after all."

"Wait a minute... You can't be saying what I think..."

"Yeah... I'm going to have to tell the only one who's been in my corner all these years that I fucked over him and his family. And he'll probably never forgive me.

Seems I'm pretty good at fucking up relationships. Who knew?" Mael downed his last shot, and with a loud clap, placed the glass on the floor beside him, mouth down. He was done. No amount of liquor would make it any better. "So before all the betrayal of Anwar, I thought about coming back, begging you to forgive me. What kind of life could we have lived, though? I am trapped in servitude as is required by the fallen. Anwar makes it look easy, but it's a penance, nonetheless. Not to mention taking care of Lelania. If I don't keep her satisfied by doing what she commands, Viktoria is going to tell one of the archangels about her, and they will end her life. Permanently. I couldn't subject you to that. So, you see... I didn't turn my back on you. I was doing it to save you from me. To save you from this life I ruined. I didn't want to add yours to my body count. You are the one person—the only person —I've ever loved just because you're you. I would have never been able to forgive myself."

This time, when he looked at her, she was staring at the floor, her body quaking from what he thought were sobs. "I would have done it... I would have helped you if only so you didn't have to deal with this on your own."

"I need to tell you one more thing." Despite her holding her hand up and shaking her head, he had confess to her. She deserved to know. "I never loved anyone else. Not since you. There's only ever been you."

"Goddammit, Mael," she said on a hiccup. "How are you even keeping yourself upright? I would have folded like a stack of cards." When she lifted her eyes, the deep brown had turned, changed into the golden-brown he remembered from all those years ago.

"Do you really want to know, or have I already lost all my cool points?"

"Yeah, seriously. How haven't you just lain down and given up?"

"You, Lily. I think of you every day and know that if I died, if I were to end it all, you would feel that. And I just couldn't bear to cause you another second of pain."

"You know, this is the absolute last thing I need to deal with right now. I can't deal with all the"—she flailed her hands again, the slight breeze she created rustling the ends of her hair—"me-and-you stuff. Let's focus. Right now, you need to deal with the most urgent thing, and that is telling Anwar. You're going to have to. Because by association, he is in danger. And if he doesn't know, he can't do anything to stop it."

She stared at him expectantly. While Mael wanted to do the right thing for the first time in his long life, he was afraid. Anwar had been the steadiest connection he'd made since he'd fallen. Their friendship through all the ups and downs had not faltered. Instead, Mael was the one who had betrayed it, and all to protect Lani. He was going to have to deal with it, sooner rather than later. "Yeah, I know."

The question was, when was the appropriate time to lose the only friend he'd had in such a very long time?

CHAPTER THIRTEEN

ANWAR

He'd wanted to check on his friend, but Mael was probably somewhere feeling low. Sometimes, it was best for males to be on their own when things were bad. Mael had caught a terrible deal with Leila. She wasn't ready to forgive him, but he wasn't ready to let go.

Anwar shook his head and left the bathroom where he'd been getting ready for bed and headed back to Farrah's side.

"You think we should call one of them? Just to be sure no one ended up in the hospital?"

"C'mon now. It's an angel and a vampire. They probably would have to do a lot of damage for one of them to be seriously in harm's way." He had to chuckle. Leila was definitely mad at Mael, but he still doubted she would gut him.

"I don't know—I've never seen her this way over any male."

"Funny, I would say the same for Mael. I haven't ever known him to be with anyone. I just kind of assumed he was private. I can understand it, considering who I was before I met you."

"Hmph, you don't say?" she said, teasing sarcasm in her tone.

"Oh, come on now. Those two are going through something unusual. Arranged marriages and whatnot are a totally different flavor. I think they just need time to talk it out."

"And there's nothing wrong with that. Listen, whatever the reason was, he is coming at her hard. I don't know if it's too much, too soon, but I do see something different in Leila."

"And what's that?"

She looked up at him as he slid under the covers and pulled her body into his. "Well, before, she never really felt anything. Maybe that's not the right way to explain it. In the past, her mask was screwed down tight. You couldn't rile her because I don't think she genuinely cared about anything beyond her immediate family—me, of course. Outside of that, she could have watched someone catch fire and wouldn't have been motivated to spit on them. She was just... kind of cold."

Folding over Farrah like a blanket, he reveled in the warmth and silky smoothness of her skin. "And you think Mael is the reason?"

"I do. I think he's changed her in just the short time they've been around one another. And it's good to see. Now, I don't know how to handle her mood swings, but I'll take this version over the last. Listless Leila has left the building. We all deserve emotions, and I would hate for her to never allow herself to *feel*."

Farrah cuddled up to him, repositioning herself until she was nearly a part of him. She seemed to love when they held one another more than anything. And whatever she wanted, she got. Most of the bedcovers, the choice of the car they drove in, and even showering first because Anwar wanted her to have every possible need met. She should never have to want for anything. If that meant he turned into the equivalent of a body pillow, then so be it.

"I know," he whispered, kissing her on her naked shoulder. "It's a shame she had to deal with so much all at once. And he isn't exactly a low-octane male. He likes being the center of attention and is always the first one to joke about something or someone. That might be over-whelming for her. I can talk to him tomorrow if you want."

Birds chirped outside the window, their makeshift perch atop the Westborn building alerting him to the morning hour coming soon. For Farrah, he'd bought blackout curtains to keep the sun out. He, as an Atlantean, did not perish in the sun like vampires, but he knew their evolutionary tradeoffs and was prepared to deal with them. For Farrah. Only for her.

"Don't bother." She glanced back at him over her shoulder. "I can't insert myself into their breakup—rather, make-up—process. They are going to do what they're going to."

"I know. I just don't want either of them to suffer..."

"Yeah, but grown folks' business is jus—"

The rattle of a cellphone vibrating against wood broke into their conversation. They both checked the night-stands on either side of the bed. It ended up being hers, and after looking at the screen, she glanced back over to Anwar. "I'm going to take this, okay? It's Ennis, and he may have a lead."

Anwar nodded and made a motion for her to go ahead and pick up. Farrah was still frowning a bit when she accepted the call and pressed the phone to her ear. "Hey. Please tell me you have something. We've been circling this thing for almost a full month." She got quiet, and Anwar could almost make out what he was saying to her. Something about there being more than one person making contact, and they had hacked into her software. There were a number of IP addresses, and that's when Ennis had lost them.

"So, can you tell who they are?"

Whatever he said brought her up onto her knees in the bed as she listened. "Okay. Well, text me the pictures and where the IP addresses are originating from. We'll check it out first thing tomorrow night. And thanks, Ennis."

Anwar made out the closing sentiment, though. Something like, "Night, gorgeous," and instantly the *kensee* in his gut roared to life. It would not be much longer before he would have to do something about their bonding. Pretty soon, he wouldn't have a choice, at least if he didn't want to end up pissing up and down the street to mark his territory. Probably an exaggeration, but to deny something his soul had destined to be his was problematic, to say the least.

"Well, does he have a lead?" Anwar skirted the issue at hand and went straight to the reason for the call.

"He does. The warehouse is for whatever they're keeping over there. There's only one male on the premises. No activity at all. I just don't get it."

"I probably need to call Mael."

"Okay. But what if he's with Leila still? The sun is coming up. I can feel it. I don't necessarily want her alone over day, either."

"Yeah, you're right. I'll text him. Tell him to meet me at nightfall."

For the first time in a while, Farrah's features relaxed a bit. It was always tough trying to figure out whether to do something to help friends when they hadn't specifically asked for assistance. Probably doubly hard with a maker and her progeny.

"Thank you," she whispered. "And I will, just for the record, let Leila know I support her decision, no matter how it turns out. Matters of the heart aren't always the most fun."

"Yup, we know that well, don't we?"

"That we do, baby. That we do," she said, and allowed herself to lie on his chest, then slipped one arm around his back and draped the other over his shoulder.

As the sun rose, Anwar pulled his female closer to him, happy he didn't have the same troubles as Mael.

CHAPTER FOURTEEN

Leila woke up hours before nightfall. She could still feel the effects of the sun, though the shields were up at VMA. At some point, after killing a fifth of whiskey, she and Mael had passed out, sprawled on top of one another, their limbs intertwined in odd positions. The years apart hadn't stopped her from seeking out his warmth over day. He'd apparently accepted her willingly since her head rested in the crook of his arm.

First, she carefully swung her leg off his back, then the other from beneath him. He was half on top of her, a strong arm around her waist securing her in place. They hadn't made it to one of the couches in the makeshift showroom that served as cover at the shop.

Finally free of their old-school Twister-like embrace, she slid away and just stared at him for a moment. She didn't need much light to see his features, thanks to her vampire sight. With a sigh, she put more distance between them. The desire to sink back into his arms was too strong to ignore when she was *that* close to him.

Oh God... what was she supposed to do with him after he confessed so much about his time away from her? Part of her understood after so many years how he struggled with even the possibility of having a relationship. The other part... well, she regretted spending all that time angry at him. Yes, she would have been hurt had she known, but she could have at least understood.

It was his fault for not trusting her to use the information wisely. He'd kind of just stuck his head in the sand and hoped for the best. Perhaps she would have handled it the same if she were in his position, but she doubted it.

Yet, for the first time, she felt like she had some culpability in the way her life had turned out. For so long, she'd blamed him for all her troubles. At any time, though, she could have just let go of the strings that tethered them together.

The hitch in her throat let her know she'd probably stumbled on some truth, whether she wanted to admit it or not. The truth was the truth, though. He'd never asked her not to live her life without him.

He had apologized for his part in all of it, but was that enough to make her forgive him? What would happen when someone else he deemed more important said they needed him? Should she be so accommodating the next time around... that is, if there was another time?

Thankfully, before she traveled too far down the path of *would've, could've, should've*, Mael stirred to life.

His head popped up, and he appeared frantic for a moment as he searched the room for her. When he laid his eyes on her, she could have sworn she heard a sigh of relief. "Good evening," he said, voice gruff with the remnants of sleep.

"Not quite," she said, not even bothering to hide the fact that she'd been staring at him.

"You know, I'd forgotten you could drink me under the table." As he attempted to push himself off the floor, he groaned a bit, which was a good indicator that he was still feeling the effects of the liquor they'd drunk. "What time is it?"

Leila glanced down at her gold Movado and found it wasn't quite seven. That time of year in Michigan, the sun was still blazing away in the sky. In a few more weeks, it would be a different story. "Six forty-nine," she said.

"Hmph, I normally don't sleep."

"Well, maybe it's just the company you're keeping these days," she said, her attempted joke feeling a little flat on her tongue.

"Yeah, well... I haven't slept in years, so perhaps that's the case."

The statement stirred in her belly. Pushing the comment—and what it did to her—aside, she picked a safer topic. "So, when are you going to tell Anwar?"

He was in the middle of peeling himself off the floor and to his feet when he looked up at her from his screwed-down brows. "Gotta give me a second to get acclimated here," he said before completing his upright motion and running a hand over lush handfuls of curls.

"I'm sorry. You're right. But it's kind of a big deal. I mean, he needs to know. And so does Farrah." She wanted to ease up, but didn't everything hinge on what he did next? Even her growing need for him. In fact, it was that need that made everything more urgent. Nothing else could be entertained until that situation was resolved.

"I'll tell him tonight. I guess getting shit off my conscience is addictive."

"I can see how that would be the case," she said. With effort, she stood up to get eye level with this male who'd managed to rip the Band-Aid from her heart and, somehow, begin the healing process in a few weeks. Wounds she'd nursed for decades were suddenly a bit smaller. If she were going to keep it real, she would have acknowledged the fact that, without those wounds, she didn't even know who she was. It was disorienting.

That was a matter for another time, however.

"Are you... I mean, do you need to, um..." He looked over at her, sheepishly at first, then with determination in his eyes. "Are you hungry?"

Shifting her weight from one side to the other, she leveled a glare at him. As much as she wanted to deny it, her fangs punched through before she could stop them, and her mouth went desert dry at the mere insinuation. Fuck, he was definitely going to see that, she thought. Still, the notion to dismiss him crossed her mind.

"It's okay. And no strings attached. I just know it's still daylight. You didn't feed yesterday... I mean, I didn't smell blood on you then. Nor when I first got here last night. I just think it's the one thing I can do for you. A peace offering. Only if you want it, though." He hadn't taken his eyes from her.

And she couldn't tear hers away, either. The truth was, she wanted to taste him again. She missed the sweetness of angelic blood on her tongue. It scared her, and simultaneously, she just wanted to get lost in him. Again. She couldn't say it, though. She couldn't let the words fall from her mouth. He was too good—at the same exact time as being too bad—for her. He was everything she wanted but couldn't have.

"It's okay," he said, before grabbing her hand and

leading her forward. He stopped in front of her favorite blue couch like he knew she needed to be somewhere she loved. Somewhere safe. Goddamn him. And she followed. She didn't pull away, didn't feign annoyance. Just... followed, as if her feet didn't belong to her anymore. As if her heart was propelling her forward and not her legs. Even as her mind protested, her body had left the station. Taking the seat, she felt the stiffness of her muscles, evidence of the internal war raging between her soul and her logic.

Mael lowered himself before her, slowly, as if waiting for her to change her mind. Placing both hands behind his back, he lay upon her lap, neck exposed to her in surrender. He handed himself over to her, and predator that she was, she knew it was the kind of thing a weaker opponent would do when the battle was lost.

With one hand, she ran her fingers through thick, coily hair then over his soft skin. Mael closed his eyes beneath her touch. It was the first time she'd allowed herself to feel him absent any pretense. Her guard dropped from her as if it were a physical wall between them, palpable like she was the one tearing the bricks down until her flesh was defenseless.

With no more inhibition, no more self-control, she lowered herself to the beating vein in his neck and sank her teeth inside.

As she broke the skin and drank, she could hear the moan coming from him as her venom mingled with his lifeforce, the intoxicating mix slipping inside him, and her being filled with the most precious gift he had to give her.

The taste of candy wine filled her mouth, and she drank deeper. She was full, but not just her appetite.

Everything about her came to life the moment she breached his barrier in every way.

"Oh, Lily... you can have me. As long as you want." The whispered words were like silk against her naked flesh, and she was more alive than she'd ever been.

The problem was, how could she possibly let him walk away from her again?

CHAPTER FIFTEEN

"She's still not answering, Anwar." To say she was worried was an understatement. They were fresh off a kidnapping, and someone had tried to hurt Farrah less than forty-eight hours before. "Did you call Mael?"

Anwar stepped into the room wearing only a white towel wrapped around him and slung low at the waist. If she weren't so nervous about Leila, she would have been properly distracted. "No, I haven't. But he always checks in with me. I'm sure they're just busy."

"Or she killed him... ever think of that? She could have killed him, and then what would we do? I'm pretty sure murdering a fallen angel would piss off the Order even more."

"Yeah, well... if she did, she would have called you to help bury the body, so we're covered there too," he said, lips turned up at the ends in amusement.

"Ha-ha. It's all fun and games until I have to borrow one of your precious cars."

"Listen, I'm fairly certain she hasn't merked my boy. If it makes you feel better, though, I'll text him. Will that work?"

"Yes, please. And I'll text Leila." Immediately, Farrah picked her phone back up off Anwar's luxe bed and tapped out a message to her liege.

Call me. Right away. I heard from Ennis.

"And also, the Order isn't too fond of Mael, so you would be off the hook there too. Shit, they might even give you a medal."

Farrah grabbed one of the pillows and chucked it at him. Because her aim was terrible, it landed on the ground some three feet away from him. "You are a trip." She laughed, despite herself.

"Yeah, I've been told. In all seriousness, are you sure they aren't just—how can I put this? Enjoying some time together?" After picking the pillow up and tossing it on the bed, he moved into the closet to grab some clothes.

"I highly doubt it. She was not exactly open to anything with him, so—"

"Well, I beg to differ."

"Why?" When he didn't say anything in reply, she raised her voice so he could hear her in the walk-in closet. The damned thing was two stories and ridiculous. "Why do you presume to know more than I do? We are best friends, and she would have told me."

A bodiless Anwar peeked his head around the corner with a smirk on his face. "Because... when they look at one another, they kind of smolder."

"I think that's the look of unadulterated hatred."

"There's a thin line between smolder and unadulterated hatred, don't you know?"

"I don't know. And honestly, like I said, I don't get into grown-ass folks' business, but she calls me. Especially since all this mess with the Order and everything else started," she said, gesturing at the world in general.

With a guffaw, Anwar dipped back into the closet. "I think I know more about organic passion than you do. You're all algorithms and matchmaking. Sometimes, people who seem the most unlikely love one another just for the fuck of it. And there is no rhyme or reason. Take the two of us. We're a little different."

Farrah, while listening to him, fell back into the covers and pulled the sheets over her naked body. She hadn't gotten dressed for the night yet, and while she should have already been in the shower, she wouldn't be able to without hearing from Leila. "How are we different?" she asked, sinking into the softness of the pillows.

"We were destined, my love. And while VMA did bring us together, I don't know that your little algorithm would have matched us. Some things are kismet. And no system can touch that."

As worried as she was, what he said shifted something inside her. She could feel her heart clutch in agreement. It was then she wrapped one of the thousand-count sheets around her and trailed into the closet behind her male. "And that, you sweet Atlantean, is why I'm lost to you." With the slide of a hand behind his neck, she pulled his head down into a kiss so deep, so passionate, she could almost feel gravity shift beneath their feet.

As if on cue, vibrations went off in the bedroom.

Reluctantly, she pulled away. Unfortunately too, because Anwar had already moved a hand to her ass and was removing the sheet with the other. "Goddammit," he whispered against her lips before she could pull away.

"I just need to—"

"Yeah, I know. But I bet it's Mael and not Leila. Only he can cockblock that well."

Farrah sprinted back across the floor to grab her cell. But it wasn't Leila... it was another number she hadn't seen in a while. Opening the text, she saw just words.

I need your help. Come alone or they'll kill me.

Eire. In another second, a map appeared on her phone. Dammit. They did have her. Farrah had known all along. She typed,

I don't know if I can just this minute. I need time to get away from everyone.

Anwar would never let it happen. Neither would Mael, who was basically for whatever Anwar was for. While she was at it, she could add Leila to that list, as well. Not to mention, she could very well be talking to someone pretending to be Eire.

There is no time.

Fuck, she needed to think. What if it *was* Eire? And if she told her own personal calvary about it, her actions could get Eire killed. She would never be able to forgive herself for that. After all, the VMA was supposed to help people.

I need proof of life.

Three dots showed up on her phone, and she waited, all the while praying Anwar didn't come out of the closet. Shit. Fuck, this was going to be a mess.

In another moment, a pic of Eire came up, her ethereal beauty disturbingly raw with bright red blotches on her forehead and deep purple bruises across one cheek.

Come. You have an hour. And remember, no one is to come with you. We have eyes everywhere.

In another minute, two more pictures popped up onscreen.

The first was of Mael and Leila. She appeared to be feeding from him, her mouth on his neck and him in a position that made him look as if he'd fallen asleep on her lap.

The next was her. Farrah was standing near a night-stand, her body wrapped in a sheet and cell phone in her right hand. Just like it was at that exact moment.

We can end everyone you love. Don't try anything bright. You don't want the kind of heat we bring.

With all of it laid out on the table, all the things she would never be able to live without at risk, there were no choices. There was no way to refuse. She sent back a message with the only option she had left.

I'll be there in an hour.

CHAPTER SIXTEEN

ANWAR

Farrah had to be truly worried about Leila because she'd torn out of there to meet her at Melody. He reminded himself when it was all over, he was going to spend hours pleasuring his female. And there was nothing and no one who would be able to stop him. Even if he had to throw both their cells off the roof of his penthouse. His cock was still hard at the thought of her.

Something about the way she'd rushed out made him immediately want to follow her. But he hadn't. She needed space. Instead, he followed up on his instincts from the morning. Something was going on with Mael, and he intended to find out what it was.

After another text, he finally got a call back a few hours later. Leaning over on the wide chair in his living room, he answered. "Hey, my man. I've been trying to get you."

"Yeah... I know. Listen, where are you? We need to talk."

"I was thinking the same. I'm home. Come on, because something has been bothering me. Probably nothing. Just need to clear the air and make sure you're good. That's all."

There was hesitation on the other line, completely unlike Mr. Quip, who always had some smart-ass reply. "I'll be there soon," Mael said just before the line went dead.

Anwar stared at his phone for a few minutes, if only to process everything that had just occurred. Mael was like another person just then, and if nothing else, it clued Anwar in that he'd been right—something was off about Mael.

Just as well they got it all out because whatever was bothering Mael was going to be nothing compared to finding those responsible for the melee surrounding VMA incidents.

When Mael didn't arrive in a few moments from wherever he was, Anwar assumed he was driving over. Since he didn't have a car, that would mean he would be with Leila and Farrah. As awkward as it may get with the females present, Mael must have been comfortable with saying whatever he needed in front of them.

Probably a good sign. As he waited, he got a shot of whiskey. Talking had never been Anwar's strong suit. He wasn't big on expressing emotions. Well, unless Farrah was involved.

She was the one exception to every single rule he'd ever had.

By the time he heard the elevator arrive on his floor,

he was another shot in and considering the next actions based on the information Ennis had provided to Farrah the night before. Whatever happened, he would end this shit soon.

"Hey," Mael said.

Anwar turned around to face his oldest friend. He'd never been big on interpersonal relationships. Before Farrah, Anwar had been somewhat of a lothario with females, standoffish with males. Funny, how far he'd come.

He found Mael cloaked in a shroud of tension and eyes filled with something that dulled the light in them. "Why do I get the feeling I'm not going to like this?"

"Because you've always been that astute."

"Where's everyone else?"

"In the car. I thought it would be best if I came up alone first. Because... I have something to tell you. And I don't want anyone hurt after I say what I have to say."

"Okay. Well, come in and spit it out, for fuck's sake. You're acting so strangely."

"Yeah, man... I just..." Mael stepped forward. "In fact, I'd better stand to tell you this."

When he didn't come forward, Anwar decided to stand, as well. Finishing off the remainder of his second shot, he placed the glass on the coffee table and covered the expanse to Mael. The fallen angel wouldn't even look at him. "What's going on, Mael?"

"I need to get this off my chest. Telling you, sharing it with Leila earlier, it puts someone at risk. Someone for whom I care greatly and would put my life on the line for again and again. So, I want you to know how important, how deadly, what I'm about to tell you is. I don't know what the outcome will be, but I couldn't live with myself if I didn't say anything."

"Go on," Anwar urged. He was growing impatient... and more nervous with every word Mael uttered.

"I haven't been honest with you. For the last few months, I've been reporting your comings and goings to Viktoria. She wants to unseat your family so that vampires can assume ranking and power since only your race and hers are founding members. She wanted to get rid of you, first because you refused to marry Eire. And then, when she discovered VMA, she urged me to push you in that direction so you'd violate the accord and give her a reason to throw the Atlanteans out of the Order." Mael's shoulders were slumped, his normally deep brown skin overcast in pallor.

It took a moment for the words to sink in. Surely, Anwar had heard incorrectly. There was no way Mael had done what he'd said, despite having admitted it. "And what the fuck am I supposed to do with this?" he asked, still in disbelief.

"I— I don't know. I just needed to tell you."

Anwar seethed. For a moment, everything around him stilled, and he could only hear the cars far below on the street as they made their way to whatever dumbass human activity they were headed to. Then, he heard Mael's heart beating in his chest. It was hard thuds, not the normal, slower cadence. "You were afraid I was about to find out, then? Is that why you're suddenly spilling your guts to me?" He practically spat the words, seemingly incapable of a civil tone.

"It's because of Azazel. He had a child, Lelania. A living Nephilim that I vowed to protect. Viktoria found out and threatened to get word to the archangels. They would kill Lelania and anyone they thought was aware of her presence. So, not only was she in danger, you and your family—"

"Nah, you sorry bastard. You don't get to do that. You don't have the right to say you did this for my family. And I don't even buy that you did this for Azazel's daughter. You fucking did this for you and that sick belief you've always held that one day the stars would align and Heaven would call you home. Well," Anwar said, shoving his hands in the pockets of his slacks to keep from throttling Mael, "I've got news for you. You are never going to get that call. If for no other reason than the fact that you ain't shit. You weren't shit for Leila. You haven't been shit for my family. And you couldn't be shit for your brethren. I don't even know why I'm surprised. It's your whole goddamned MO, isn't it?"

Mael didn't say anything for a moment. With his lips pressed thin, he held his head down, eyes on the floor. He seemed to grow smaller before Anwar, his body closing in on itself. "I deserve that."

"You're damn right you deserve it. Ain't that a bitch? You were supposed to be serving a penance. Or did you forget that too?"

"I have never once forgotten my obligations. I thought no one knew. I thought I could keep Lelania concealed. I would have never—"

"Ah, see that's where you're wrong. You did."

"I— I did. It was wrong of me, but I need to tell you, Nephilim are the most hated evidence of the fallibility of angels. They are hunted, eradicated. As far as I know, Lani is the only one that ever resulted in a live birth. She dies every fifty years, so I am responsible to exhume her and to find her another family every time—"

"Look at me, Mael," Anwar demanded. When he didn't raise his eyes, he used more force. "Fucking look at me." This brought his head up. "Do you think I give one fuck about some dead angel's bastard when her existence is what put me and mine in danger? Huh?"

"I think you would if you weren't so angry right now."

"And if you had told me all this before, I could have made decisions. I could have helped you. But you chose not to."

"I did. And I'm very sorry. But I was doing what I thought was best under the circumstances. Since that time, I have seen the error of my ways."

"What happened? Leila called you on your bullshit?"

"No. Actually, she did insist I tell you sooner rather than later. But I had resolved I was going to tell you by then. I am a man of my word. An angel of the Lord—"

"Ex. You are an *ex*-angel, Mael. The sooner you accept that shit, the better off you'll be. Hell, maybe if you'd accepted it in the first place, you wouldn't have judgment so cloudy it resembles swamp water."

"Yes, I am aware. I don't expect you to forgive me for my indiscretions. I am sure it would be too much to ask. I just didn't want you to think I disappeared without telling you why. I'm sure once Viktoria tells the angels, I will be out of your hair swiftly."

"I didn't expect anything less. That's what you're good at, after all. Fucking up, then leaving."

"Yeah, Anwar. If you want to believe that, then go ahead. I can't stop you. All I can say is I didn't mean for any of this to happen. It's unfortunate. And after so many years, I am just as disheartened as you. So, I'll go now, but just know, I am truly sorry. I hope one day you can believe me."

"Yeah, whatever." Anwar cursed under his breath. It was more from the stabbing pain of betrayal in his chest than from the news Mael had just laid on his lap. He would have understood if Mael had come to him before. The problem was Mael's omission.

Just as Anwar was about to turn his back to his ex-confidant, the doorbell chimed. Anwar didn't stop his stride to the windows overlooking the Ambassador Bridge. For the first time, he imagined hanging Mael's ass up there by his fucking wings.

"Hi, Anwar. Everything okay?"

Anwar didn't turn around to look at Leila, though he knew she was the one who'd entered.

"Fucking awesome. I mean, really. When everything else is jacked, why not do a pile-on situation and go for the gusto?" No one said anything, and it wasn't until Anwar turned around that white, abject horror struck like lightning throughout his body. "Where is Farrah?"

"Oh, I don't know. I thought she was here, so I was coming up to see how she was dealing with the news." Leila looked between the two of them as reality started to settle in.

None of them had any idea where Farrah was.

"She told me she was meeting you at Melody. Did your wires get crossed or something?"

"Well, I texted her back after I didn't get an answer from her. Since we were on the way, I just decided to wait to speak to her."

Anwar's head swam as he ran their last exchange through his mind. Farrah, after she'd replied to the last text, had hurriedly gotten dressed, damn near using vampire speed, and bolted out of the door.

"They have her," he said. There was no evidence to support his theory, but he would bet on it.

"What do you mean?" Leila asked, fresh panic in her voice.

"I mean, they have her. I'm not sure what they did, but I know she wouldn't have lied to me unless it was for a good reason. I'm going to get her," Anwar said, practically flying from the room.

"We're coming with you," Leila called out.

Footfalls sounded out behind Anwar as he made his way to the lift. "No, you call Ennis and have him text whatever he sent Farrah last night. I'm going to take care of this on my own. I can't trust others, nor do I have any interest in doing so."

"Anwar, we are coming. Whether you want help or not, we're taking your six."

He couldn't hit the elevator button before a thick hand reached around him and jabbed it.

"I don't have time to fuck around with you two on this. But you stay out of my fucking way, you got me?" he barked. Pulling a hairband from his pocket, he bound his locs into a half bun at the nape of his neck and stripped the jacket and button-down shirt off, leaving him in only a T-shirt, fitted slacks, and shoes that were probably not the best choice for what he was about to do to whoever had Farrah. None of it mattered. He would decapitate him. Or them. "I'm going to end this tonight. They will never take her from me again."

When the doors opened, Anwar stepped in first and then waited for his unwanted companions before turning the key to lock things down.

No matter how long it took, wherever they were holding her, Anwar was going to find them, then rip them new assholes. Then he would deal with Mael's betrayal.

Not a moment before he had his beloved back at his side.

CHAPTER SEVENTEEN

Of all the things Mael regretted, the worst was hurting the two individuals who meant the most to him. Anwar had been right about a lot of what he'd said, but he was wrong about one crucial, universal truth.

Mael hadn't truly given a fuck what happened to himself. He was ready to deal with the consequences of his actions years ago. He'd always known an archangel would come and take him out. Something about living on borrowed time made him immune to the invincible fallacy. He wasn't invincible, nor had he expected to be able to keep up his protection of Lani for even one of her lifecycles. Surely, some overzealous angel would one day pick up on her heat signature, and it would all be over. They would test her, find out who had fathered her, and that would be the end of it.

He'd never had any delusions about his own life being long and healthy. Everything he'd done had been because he was trying to save those he'd been bound to. Maybe one day, he would get a chance to explain that to Anwar. But it wouldn't be today.

For today, he would help Anwar save the one he had come to love. And if that wasn't enough to prove Mael's loyalty, then Mael would live with it. When they ended the matter at hand, then Mael would deal with Viktoria. One way or another. He could have killed her long ago, but it had been his penance, the demand that the fallen live in servitude for the rest of their lives. Which was intended to be a good, long time. Then, once their debts were paid, they were to surrender their wings and live among the human souls as one of them.

He would be headed in the other direction. But not regular Hell. It would be one specially designed for angels who wound up there.

"How much farther?" Leila's voice cut into his thoughts. She was driving erratically, which was understandable based on the address Ennis had texted.

"GPS says we have about two minutes. Should be just up ahead on Second Avenue." They'd decided to drive since there was no way to tell what condition Farrah would be in. Hell, there was no way of knowing if she was there.

Leila didn't say anything, merely nodded.

Anwar had chosen to fly, apparently unable to bear being in the car with Mael, which was understandable. He was angry with him, and it was his right, given Mael's actions. He would grant him the space he needed to work through whatever he was feeling.

"She's going to be okay," Mael whispered. "She has to be."

"She'd better be. There's no one left, Mael. I don't have anyone," Leila said. He was sure it was an automatic response since she was hyper-focused on the road ahead of her.

Soft rain fell outside, glittering atop the asphalt. The tires on Leila's '71 GTO were squeaking on the blacktop with every turn she took. The engine strained under the demand she was placing on the old-school car.

Upon arrival, they parked across from the warehouse. It was in a fairly barren area of the city. There were several neighborhoods on the eastside in a similar state. Developers were buying the old buildings and clearing them out along the way. Since there weren't many upgrades made that Anwar could see, the warehouse must have been a holdover by whoever owned it. Since Farrah's capturers had been using it as a refuge, that could have been the reason.

By the time Mael closed the car door, Anwar was landing in the lot to the right of the warehouse, a vacant property overgrown with weeds and wildflowers. He walked over to them but only looked at Leila, who had armed herself with an electric cattle prod. "I'm going to start on the top. You go in through the back door," he directed.

"No, Leila isn't going in first. It'll be me. And I know you're pissed at me, but I will not endanger her. I won't let anyone else do it, either," Mael said, a snap in his tone. He would still shut down the world for her. It was non-negotiable.

"Fine. Just stay out of my way," Anwar barked before taking off. It was one giant leap to the roof of the warehouse.

Mael watched until he got up there then motioned for Leila to follow him. She hadn't said anything about him speaking up for her, and he hoped she didn't. If he had his way, he would always defend her, even if she didn't think she needed it. Undoubtedly, he would hear about it later.

Now was the time for putting an end to the extraneous bullshit of some sick fucker.

As they made their way around the building, Mael was on the lookout for lights and movement within the darkened windows. There was no one walking around that he could see.

On the porch, he stripped off his white shirt and let it fall to the damp ground. Keeping his wings in close, he tested the doorknob to see if it was locked. When he found it was, he squeezed until the dingy golden handle crumpled in his hand and fell to the ground in pieces. Motioning to Leila to stay put, he pushed in on the door. Peeling paint left little more than termite-ridden wood exposed. They stepped into a darkened area. As the floorboards accepted his weight, they groaned beneath his feet. It was then he felt the warding. His power would be somewhat diminished. *Shit...*

He wished it wasn't such a tight space because he would have used his wings. Their seven-foot span wouldn't allow it in here. Not easily anyway. So he would have to do what was needed without them.

He moved slowly through the old factory-turned-warehouse. Empty boxes and the stench of decaying rodents were all that remained. But, beyond the warding, something else about it wasn't quite right.

He motioned for Leila to come inside before slowly making his way to the basement stairs. And then he noticed it. About the time Anwar came around the corner from searching upstairs.

The door to the lower level had a brand-new, shiny stainless-steel lock on it. Probably the only thing from the twenty-first century on the entire property.

It was a shitty location for vampires, so it all made

sense. Put Farrah in the basement away from the sun. What didn't make sense was why they had her in the first place.

"Downstairs," he mouthed. All of them could see exceptionally well given their supernatural abilities. There was no way to know who was lurking in there, and he wasn't willing to take the chance on Farrah's life, or Eire's, for that matter.

Anwar stepped forward, taking the lock in his hand, but immediately, he jumped away, holding his hand as the scent of burning flesh rose in the air.

Silver.

"Fuck these bastards," Anwar whisper-yelled while holding his hand to his chest.

Mael took that as a cue to remove the lock. In seconds, he had the thing off and the door open. Anwar barged forward without waiting. When Leila took a step forward, Mael pulled her back. "Together. Eyes on me. And there's warding, so I may not be as strong here. No way to tell until we're in it," he advised.

She nodded in agreement again, eyes wide and on him. At least she was trying to keep herself safe. The truth was, if something were to happen to her, he would lose his shit. In that, he understood what Anwar was going through. To lose a mate was devastating. And as such, he made a personal vow to get Farrah back. While they weren't mated yet, it was a foregone conclusion they would be in the future. Even if they didn't know it yet.

The descent into the basement was long, much longer than one would expect. Mael didn't dare flip on his cell for light to see the walls around them with a bit more clarity. Instead, he just used the resources available to him.

The temp dropped the deeper they went. There was

a faint scent of mold and moist earth, which meant someone had dug the hole recently and hadn't put any more concrete on the walls. Whoever it was had gone to a great deal of trouble to build out a subterranean level perfect for keeping hostages or prisoners.

It would explain why Ennis's surveillance hadn't been able to find any people.

Finally, after they'd turned a corner and dropped another hundred feet or so down, an entrance opened up before them. Heightened vision afforded him some clarity in the darkened interior, but not much. Mael could smell the salt that ran beneath the city of Detroit. That's how deep they were into the earth.

Anwar turned slightly on the narrow stairs. Holding two fingers toward himself and then pointing at Mael, it was a warning to stay aware.

He replied with a stiff nod and glanced behind him to the one who mattered most at the moment. Leila's eyes were wide and aware. She hadn't missed a beat, and though Mael would have preferred to not have her there due to the distraction, the feeling of them relying on one another was pure bliss. Their lockstep movement, her so close to him he could smell her scent as more than just a memory, pushed every other bad thing that had happened from his mind. After all, if he weren't in this situation, he wouldn't have her back in his life, for however long it lasted this time. Mael was ready to accept his fate with Anwar, with the Order, and with the angels. If Leila wasn't going to be a part of his life anyway, then what did it matter?

They were close to the bottom, Mael could sense. There was a persistent dripping sound coming closer with every step they took, and he wondered if they were all walking into a trap. With that came a dread he couldn't shake.

On the ground, his vision adjusted to the next-level darkness into which they had descended. The three of them spread out, searching the space so cavernous, it must have taken an army of humans to hollow it out. There were doors leading to who-knew-where before them. Thanks to his heightened vision, he could make them out. Either the effects of whatever spellwork was at play or the material they were constructed of prevented his ability to hear movement or sound on the other side. It could have been anything, but there was only one way to find out. And that was to go through them.

Anwar stepped forward first, and Mael reached behind him to find Leila, but she'd moved off to one of the doors.

"Leila..." he whispered urgently.

She waved him off and kept moving forward. Mael was hot on her heels, his hackles on ten, and a sudden awareness they weren't alone.

He couldn't see anyone but knew they were there. The blessing that was his angel perception fired alarms that went to his soul. "You may as well show yourself," he called out.

He heard a groan from his right and saw Leila suddenly lurch forward at the same time as the room was flooded with bright light from everywhere, so blinding, it was as if they were being X-rayed. Disorienting, arresting, and panic-inducing. Half-blind, he stumbled toward Leila in time to catch her before she fell forward. "Anwar," he screamed out. He grabbed her body on the way down and heard the clinking of metal hit the ground. Undoubtedly, she hadn't been able to hang on to her weapon given how limp she felt in his arms.

There was wetness on her shirt. He could feel the same warm dampness on his belly as she listlessly tumbled against him.

As his vision came back online, he saw the most horrible sight. His love, Leila, staring up at him vacantly. She'd been staked. "No, fucking no!" he cried out.

Anwar stood beside him, his eyes holding the same shock and horror Mael felt.

A small, weak voice emanated from behind one of the doors—Farrah, but Mael couldn't track it. Everything inside him shattered as Leila's precious blood spilled over him, over the floor. Splinters poked at his fingers as he stroked her back and collapsed to the floor with his love in his arms.

On the ground, he had one thought. One singular focus that took over every part of his being. If this was the end of her, then it would be the end of every single being involved, if it took him the rest of his life.

CHAPTER EIGHTEEN

ANWAR

nwar lost all sense of time and space as he watched Leila bleed out, then heard his love from somewhere beyond one of those doors. Someone had done that to Leila and was probably still in the room, but he couldn't focus on anything until he found Farrah.

She'd cried out for him, a sickeningly weak tone in her voice.

"Farrah," he yelled, waiting a moment to hear from where she'd called to him, to be sure he could find her. He reached out, trying to locate her using the blood in her body. There was an echo, a calling that normally would be clear. The connection was muddied by the anxiety surging within him.

"I'm here..." Her disembodied voice was so faint, he knew she was hurt. Knew she was in pain.

There. The middle door was where she was. With everything inside him, he charged it, his feet digging into the dirt floor as he pressed against the barrier to his female. With a roar that brought down clumps of dirt around him, he backed away then charged it again, this time sending shock waves of pain that didn't register. Adrenaline fueled him. Desperation kept him power-driving that door until it splintered. When he got in... Oh God...

In the center of the floor, Farrah was tied to a chair, her curly hair matted with blood and who knew what else, a nasty slash across her face. Her head lolled to the side, her mouth slack and working as if trying to manage words but not quite able to.

"Farrah," he said, his body moving on its own. Hearing and all neuro reception fizzled out in a loud clap and buzz in his ears. He was on his knees and unsure of whether he walked over and lowered his body to her or if he fell face-first into her.

His hands moved to her ropes and shook as he clawed at the knots binding her wrists, then her ankles. He worked without looking at them, unable to take his eyes off her face. He wanted to ensure she remained conscious. "Stay with me, baby. I need you, okay? Okay?" The voice was foreign in his ears, unsure of whether his hearing was blown out from the stress of the situation or if he'd actually been reduced to the whimpering mess he sounded like.

"Ai-air..." she said on a ragged breath.

"I know, I— I'm going to get you up outside..." Finally, the stubborn ropes came undone in his clumsy fingers.

"No... it's Eire... She did this t-t-to me..." she said, coughing on the words.

Fuck. Tarik's daughter? How the fuck was she involved? Suddenly, everything made sense. The wound

Leila had sustained, the break-in at Farrah's, all would have needed to happen without the benefit of being visible, and the fae had the ability to cloak themselves. The spellwork limiting Mael's powers and the ability for her to sneak up on them while cloaked explained how she was doing it.

The *how* fit, but the *why* of it was not so easily understood. That was something that stumped Anwar, but the muddled state of his brain was consumed by getting Farrah out of there. Leila too. And there was bound to be someone else in the underground lair. There was no way Eire was working alone. "Mael, you need to watch out for Eire. She's here," he yelled to ensure Mael heard him.

He heard stumbling behind him and immediately inhaled an aroma that made his blood run cold. It was the coppery tinge of blood carried along on Leila's scent.

"I figured. It would need to be someone with the power of invisibility. And she's still around," Mael said, standing beside him as Anwar lifted Farrah off the chair and laid her out on the floor. Her body jerked from the movement, little moans escaping her as he let her down as gently as he could. She'd been staked too, like Leila, and it had left a wicked tear that went straight through her body. "I need to get her out of here... Leila too."

"Yeah, I'm aware. You go, and I'll deal with this shit. But you have to take both of them," Mael barked.

"They're going to be in a lot of pain going up those stairs." He glanced over at Leila.

Her mouth was slack, her eyes open but staring at nothing. He could hear her taking ragged breaths. Oxygen and blood would increase her healing, so she would need both. To get neither would most assuredly seal her fate. She was barely hanging on. Once on the surface, he would need to be able to take care of her blood needs. Something told him, though, if Mael found out he'd fed his female, it would be an entirely different problem. As pissed as he was with Mael and his actions, he didn't want to punish him in that way.

"I need you to feed Leila," Anwar said.

"No, go. I will deal. Just get them out of here. I can feel the presence of more of these bastards, coming in hot."

"I don—"

"No, Anwar, please don't think. Just take them and go."

He hated to do it, but it was necessary. There were going to be so many debts due at the end of this thing, but they would have to figure it out later. And hopefully, they would all make it out alive.

CHAPTER NINETEEN

ael and Anwar carried their females back to the entryway. For some reason, Eire hadn't made herself visible just yet. The fucking warding inhibited his ability to sense movement. But Mael knew there would be no way to find her with half of his energy focused on Leila. Anwar needed to get her out of there if she was going to have a chance at healing. As resilient as vampires were, there would be no recovery from a gaping wound in the middle of the sternum without blood.

If she died, Mael would never get the chance to make amends with the woman he loved. The fact alone made everything, all of it, meaningless.

"Can you manage the logistics of this, man?" Mael asked as he waited for Anwar to shift Farrah's body over his shoulder.

"I'm going to have to, aren't I? They won't make it if I don't."

It was a grim outlook, something that would leave both of them broken shells of their former selves. Mael knew it, and based on the look in his eyes, Anwar knew it, as well.

Mael couldn't reply. It was going to be bloody and gruesome making it up all those stairs. Instead, he nodded and stepped forward. He helped Anwar position the females, each of them groaning in agony as their weight was redistributed over Anwar's broad shoulders. They would likely feel every step he took up the hundreds of stairs and out onto the street. Thank God they'd driven. Hopefully, Anwar would be able to get them far away from their current hellscape. "Be careful, brother."

"Yeah... you too," Anwar said.

Mael pressed his back against the ragged jamb of the entryway and stood there until he could no longer see Anwar's back as he ascended the stairs. Despite the added weight of Farrah and Leila, he was able to rise quickly. Not as fast as his normal pace, but still rapid, considering. It was a relief, and though Mael knew the pain for both women would be great, it would be over sooner rather than later. He just prayed none of his and Anwar's efforts were too little, too late.

With a turn, he stalked back into the now brightly lit interior of the cave. "Eire, you might as well show your-self. We know it's you. And whoever else you have with you."

"You act like you have a leg to stand on here. Can't you see when you're outgunned, Foghorn?"

"Who put you up to this?" he growled, trying to follow the sound of the disembodied voice.

"Isn't that just like a male? Thinking females need someone to mastermind their plans because they are weak and incapable. No, no... this was all me. I'm not sure how you thought I would take being jilted practically at the altar by Anwar, but that should have been a consideration. I've watched you all bumbling around for weeks. Thinking it was Viktoria, the bitch. She ruined me. No respectable fae male will take a jilted princess, I don't care how dazzling I look. Everyone knew Anwar opted out of our mating. It was a poor reflection on me in the end. But he didn't give a damn about that, did he? Fuck him. Screw all of them, the bastards. The Order believes they can move us around like pawns on a chessboard when they are nothing but liars and thieves, one step away from savages themselves. Who are they to rule over us?"

A tap on Mael's shoulder, light as a feather, brought him pinwheeling around only to meet nothingness. He growled, frustration with the female mounting.

"Nope, I was sitting there with my thumb up my pretty ass when, one day, I overhead Viktoria's conversation with, of all people, Maelstrom. I thought to myself, couldn't be. Would they be collaborating behind Anwar's back?"

"Fuck you for this, Eire. You and your entire clan will pay for this treachery."

"You seem to think you all are going to get out of this, somehow. I guess I can't blame you for wishful thinking. But the car you drove here? All flat tires. Upstairs, there are three shifters waiting for Anwar. You probably missed them because I slipped them a bit of my blood. Funny thing about the fae... we can loan out our powers, so to speak. The metamorphosis is quite effective."

With every word she uttered into the listless atmosphere, Mael's resolve sank a bit lower.

"And one more thing, Mael. That stake didn't go through Leila's heart on purpose. I wanted her to feel every bit of the poison I tainted it with as she slips away into nothingness. And get this. The only cure is in what? Fae blood, save a miracle. So unless you have Tinkerbell in your goddamned pocket, she is... oh shit, what's the human phrase? DOA? Something like that." A maniacal laugh flooded the space.

The roar that emanated from him was foreign, more monster than his angelic nature. The earthen walls around them trembled, his vocal cords straining against the makeshift rafters as all the pain, frustration, and agony poured from him. Anger forced him to lash out, at the air, the earth, whatever was around him. It was then he felt it. The razor-sharp edge of his wing clipped something, and a splatter of blood hit the wall.

At once, Eire materialized before him, her smug arrogance slowly draining from her face. She'd been hit and held her hand over the open wound in her side. With a step back, she pointed to Mael. "What are you waiting for? Get him," she screamed at her invisible helpers.

Mael glared at the recently materialized pair of foot soldiers running in his direction. One was a human male he didn't know, and the other, Billy McDermott. Billy had been the one Mael and Anwar had originally assumed was behind everything.

The humans had no way of attaining such skills unless Eire had loaned them some of her powers. There were two ways to do this—by sharing blood or the much more temporary solution of enchanting them with spellwork. It didn't last for very long, but enough time to, say, break into an apartment or disappear inside a warehouse.

Fuck him forever, Eire had been the mastermind.

Mael didn't move, simply waited for them as he assessed their individual weaknesses. Billy was obviously right-handed, as he leaned forward favoring that direction. He'd most likely align his eyes to show exactly where he planned to land a punch. The other was like a baby gazelle, running in and mimicking the movements of his partner. He was young, flailed a lot. Mael was quite sure these two would be dead in the next few minutes.

Regardless of whether they were supernatural or human, there was one surefire way to end it. He would rip their heads from their shoulders before they took their next breath.

As he'd expected, the first was supposed to be the leader—fucking Billy. He launched in, right flank first, leaving his ribcage exposed. The first punch went exactly where the lug's eyes focused, a headshot that Mael easily ducked before leaning in with a soft-paw punch that sank in as he executed—the sound like a piece of wood breaking.

His opponent went down on one knee with a grunt. Mael immediately followed up with a roundhouse kick to the head, taking him completely out. In one lunge, he straddled Billy's torso, and with both hands on either side of his neck, he pulled, wrenching until flesh gave way, the thing popping off with a sloppy gush of blood that ended up splattered over Mael's chest. He threw it across the floor. Billy's melon landed at Eire's feet, followed by a plume of dust from the dirt floor. She stepped back as if to avoid ruining her thousand-dollar shoes, whatever those red-bottomed things were called. Mael mentally promised he would rip those bitches off her feet and burn them.

"C'mon," he said to the remaining flunky while motioning for him to come forward with one hand. He could see the fear in the youngster's eyes. There was no way he was going to let Leila being hurt slide, even for some kid playing follow the leader or trying to get whatever prize Eire had promised him. Could have been a million dollars, or it could have been a roll in the sack. Whatever it was, Mael was about to make sure the boy knew it hadn't been worth it.

He was taller than Billy, staring at Mael eye to eye as he stepped into what had become Mael's ring of death. The splattering of blood pooled around his feet, and Mael stepped over the headless body to get closer to the youth. Ah, but he'd been wrong about one thing. The kid hadn't backed down, but that didn't mean he wasn't afraid. Fear had a stench. Like rotting garbage, it rolled from him. There was no mistaking it, and Mael remembered it from his days of fighting on the side of Heaven. It was the same stench that came off the demons moments before he tore them apart with his bare hands.

The kid put up his hands as if he was about to enter a prizefight. He must have been trained for human boxing. Clearly, he'd never fought an archangel. No matter how long Mael had been fallen, he would never forget his training. And it was coming back to him—the vicious kills and the absence of humanity. Still fit like a goddamned glove.

"What are you waiting for? You're doing all that dancing around, and I gotta be honest, you aren't exactly my type," he said, laughing after his own joke. There was a certain mania that came with unbearable grief. Mael had leaned straight into it.

"You think you're funny, huh?" the kid said through gritted teeth. Now that he was closer, Mael saw he couldn't have been more than late-twenties.

Before, Mael would have at least felt a little bad about killing him. "Oh, I think I'm hilarious. But what's funny is, it's not me with the humor. It's you. You let this little girl get you hyped up to believe you would be a match for me? And for what? A taste of glory? I'll tell you something, boy. This is not going to go the way you thought. And what's worse? We could have been on the same team, if only your girl here would have left me and mine out of her shit since I hate the Order as much as she does."

"That so?" In his gangly way, the boy took a sloppy punch and nearly fell on his face since his weight distribution was uneven as Mael moved past the slow punch.

Turning slightly, he slapped him on the back of his head, behind him so fast, the poor boy didn't have time to think. "*Tsk.* That's a shame. Whoever trained you didn't tell you how to control your punches. Might have been more impactful to use the windmill... remember, the one baby girls do in kindergarten?"

"Fuck you," the male spat out. He was turning red, his pale skin flushed with both exertion and frustration.

"No, no... my friend. I think you're the one who's fucked." Tired of the cat-and-mouse, he stepped into his opponent's weak side, this time on the left. With a three-punch combo, head-head-body shot, he had the young cub off balance. He followed up with two more jabs to the mouth and nose. The boy did end up in that pinwheel, pivoting backward as he lost control of his body.

Eire's boy toy fell onto his back, the hollow sound of the wind being knocked out of him coming seconds later. "*Ooph...*"

"Yeah, I know." Mael moved to stand over his latest victim. "Sucks to have your last sight be a pissed-off angel when they tell you we're supposed to be all grace and peace. Nobody seems to remember the other stories. The ones where we are vengeance and acrimony." Before the cub could respond, one sharp edge of Mael's wing was across his neck. His mouth was still working in an unspoken cry as his tendons, bone, and cartilage were severed. A crimson pool formed quickly beneath the dead, twitching body.

Slowly, Mael raised his eyes to the last remaining being who'd harmed his Lily.

The truth was, Mael didn't care if he won, didn't care about anything in that moment. Anger fueled him, agony from his heart shattering into a thousand pieces made him mourn the life he'd dreamed of and would never get to live. Those two emotions alone informed his actions—not his mind, not instincts. Only a blind fury was left. As he stalked toward Eire, this female, he didn't think of her powerful father, nor that she was truly out to get him. Instead, he only saw Lily's murderer.

Lily... the female he'd never be able to repay for all the pain he'd caused her, no matter how long he lived. Mael had turned away when he should have been her safe harbor. It was something he would have to recall for the rest of his life. From the sincerest place in his soul, he hoped he would die tonight. Perhaps Eire would kill him. If only so that he didn't have to face a world without Lily in it.

"Mael, you aren't thinking straight," Eire said. She was wounded, which was probably the only reason she wasn't able to cast her disorienting spell over him. Even with the warding in place, she most likely couldn't focus. "I have a proposition for you... think of it. We could take down those who oppress us together. I know you. You haven't gotten a fair shake. Viktoria drove a wedge between you and Anwar. Wouldn't you love to get revenge on her too?"

The sardonic laugh wasn't one Mael could control. "You think I need your help, girl?"

"Anyone ever tell you using pronouns to address someone is misogynistic as fuck?" With Mael inches away from her, she faded into nothingness.

Of course, she did. It was probably the only power of hers that still worked with the gash cut into her stomach from Mael's wing. "I don't need to see you to kill you, Eire," he said, spinning on his heel and screaming into the void, the sound echoing off the dark steel rafters.

"Don't you, though?" The disembodied voice bounced around, coming from everywhere at once.

"You'd be surprised by what I can do."

"And when I'm done with you," she continued, seemingly ignoring Mael's assertion, "I'm going to ruin Anwar and his boo. How could he believe that plain Jane was a better option than me? The audacity. And to think, if he had played his cards right, he could have had both of us."

"You need to be mindful of who you're speaking to, girl." That time, it was just to piss her off.

"I think you've got that wrong. Mael, you're just Constantine and Anwar's lapdog. The only reason the Order tolerated you at all was because of your proximity to the Atlanteans. And if I'm not mistaken, you know it too."

"That's it? You think your little insults can get under my skin?"

"No, but this can…"

A wave of heat swept over Mael's body. The pain started in his side, and when he touched there, it was wet. With his blood. Goddammit, it stung. "You bitch," he sputtered, his jaw clamped tight from the pain.

"Oh no. There it is. The patriarchy on full display.

Ready to compare any female who proves to be too much of a handful to a four-legged beast."

Mael focused on her voice. Though his side felt like a million shards of hot glass burrowed into his flesh, he struggled to trace her. She was circling, like a shark toying with wounded prey. "Yeah, this has been fun," he said, "but I'm going to have to get off your delusional train now."

"I bet you'd like to. Know what that searing-hot pain is? I hit you with liquid iron. You should feel it entering your bloodstream. I guess I could have stabbed you, but I like to play with my food a little."

"Just sick..." Mael took a step but fell to the floor. His leg gave way. Paralysis was a symptom of blood poisoning.

"Whew, this is fun. The great Mael, slowly dying. Something hundreds of demons tried back in the good old days, and you're taken out by little old me. What was it that you called me? A bitch? *Hmph*... I guess I am, after all."

Mael watched as Eire made herself corporeal before him. "This is going to end badly for you," he said, gasping as his tongue thickened. A strong metallic taste filled his mouth, and he wondered how soon it would be, if he could hope to see his Lily again where he was going. Of course, he should have been fighting the effects, but it was what he'd wanted, right? Not to face the bitterness of the world if he couldn't have her...

"Oh, c'mon, Mael." Using her snakeskin stiletto, Eire kicked him as he lay on the floor at her feet. "This is not fun at all. You're just giving up. I can feel it. The will to live draining from you. I thought you would at least go out like a warrior. Instead, you're more like a slug. Just laid out there, letting your angel grace—or whatever the fuck it's called—drain into the dirt. Ugh, I can't stand it. No wonder they booted your ass out of Heaven."

"You know what's sadder"—Mael coughed—"you're doing all this because no one wants you. Not Anwar, not your dad. Talk about daddy issues. It's funny because don't girls like you end up married to some replica of their father? You should be three pups in by now."

"You really are a dick, aren't you?"

Another blinding boot to the head followed, sending Mael's melon rocking off to the side—that time his own blood spilled over his chest.

"I take back everything I said. You should die like a slug. A nothing-ass fallen with no honor, no soul."

"See now, that's where you're wrong. I had a soul. You killed her." He spat blood out of his mouth, the deep red dribbling onto his arm.

"Oh my God, *waaa*. You're like a toddler over her. Women are a dime a dozen for a stud like you. And just so you know, she wasn't even into you."

"On second thought, I think I will just go ahead and take you out. And I hate those fucking shoes, by the way. Anyone ever tell you following trends makes you basic?"

Mael rocked his body up on his forearm only to be kicked in the stomach. The pain was like a vise grip across his midsection, and for all his talk, he wasn't going to be able to kill her.

Oh yeah, that last insult was probably a bad idea. But if he was going to go out, it might as well be as the bastard he'd always been.

CHAPTER TWENTY

*A*nwar was taxed upon reaching the top of the stairs. There was no way he would make it to the car, and based on the amount of blood on the back of his shirt, he knew he had to stop and give Farrah and Leila blood.

He searched the room to see if anyone else was there. When he found no one, he moved to the couch he would have never even stood beside before but now was exactly what he needed to get them the vital blood they would need to recover before it was too late.

He laid them down as gently as he could with both his hands occupied. As pained as their collective groans were, the floor would have been worse, although he couldn't imagine it would have possibly been any dirtier. As their weight hit the tattered material, an aroma that must have been akin to the bowels of Hell hit him in the face.

Immediately, he went to work. Taking his own fangs and ripping his forearm open, he cupped Farrah's face and leaked his blood into her mouth. When she swallowed once, he tried to do the same for Leila.

Instantly, her body seized, teeth clenched, and she sputtered.

"Goddammit," he hissed. Leaning forward, he pulled his belt free and tried to slip it into her mouth. He'd read somewhere that it was important to keep the tongue out of the way so that they didn't injure themselves beyond repair. He forced it between her teeth.

"Anwar..." A hazy moan came from Farrah. "What... wh—"

"Shhhh, don't try to talk." Once the belt was in place and clamped between fangs and teeth, he held Leila's torso in place with one hand and bit into his other forearm, placing it over Farrah's mouth.

The sting of her ferocious bite rippled through his entire body, and he stiffened in an involuntary reaction. She drank and drank, but Leila... She didn't stop convulsing. "I've got to get y'all out of here," Anwar said, glancing around again for something to possibly carry Leila on. The hope was that Farrah could garner enough strength to help hold Leila upright as her body continued to buck out of control. "Shit..."

Scanning the room again, he saw it. A flicker from the streetlight outside. Then heard the movement. Someone was there. He had to practically rip his arm from Farrah as he got to his feet and turned in time to see a hulking shifter still in human form coming up with something in his hand. Small and slightly concealed, he hadn't realized what it was before the slice left his arm gaping open.

Catching his attacker's hand with the knife before he

could fully complete his swing, Anwar snatched him forward with as much strength as he could muster. The pop and crunch, followed by a howl that would wake dead souls, let Anwar know he'd broken his wrist. Not stopping, he followed through with a punch to the male's face. Anwar wasn't sure whether the blood splatter that hit him was from the shifter's nose or if the tears in his arms were leaking. And it didn't matter.

As his assailant went down, Anwar took his booted foot and pressed it into his twisted torso, stomping him into the ground while pulling at that arm. A chorus of yelps rang out, but between the moaning, he heard a growling behind him.

Before he could turn, he felt the weight of a Mack truck, smelled the wet-dog scent of a freshly transformed wolf on his back, then, in a moment of sheer anguish, white-hot pain flooded him as gnashing teeth sank into his neck.

He was down, on top of the other shifter, and bending his arm ninety degrees in the wrong direction. With one wolf below him and another on top, he could feel the vibrations of a pending shift below him.

He was probably going to die. Imminently. "Farrah, take Leila and go," he yelled, all the while struggling to get the dank-smelling beast off his back.

"I can't," she cried out, the sound of distress breaking in her voice on the ends of her words.

Anwar shimmied his hands free and beat at the snarling wolf still locked down on his neck, but the force he needed wasn't there. His vision speckled, and he knew, in another few moments, he would be out. And Farrah, and the other person closest to her, would be right behind him.

In an instant, the wolf released him. A whimper sounded out behind him. The weight lifted from his body, and there was no way his assailant had changed his mind. Pushing off the other shifter, he managed to roll himself onto his back in time to find a... a woman. His fleeting senses told him she was human, but how could that be? The shifter had to weigh at least three hundred pounds, and there was no way she would have been able to snatch him up like that. Not a human, and for the most part, not many of the supernatural females he knew of could pull off such a feat.

"Stay down. I need to help her first," she said. She was a tall Black woman, her features modest, her aura calming.

Anwar couldn't nod or even speak in that moment. He was still losing so much blood from his neck wound, and one side of his body had gone numb. But he knew one thing. He needed to end the shifter next to him. Feeling around on the floor, he found the knife that had been in the shifter's hand and plunged it into his forehead. The blade vibrated in his palm as it cut through flesh and penetrated bone. Immediately, he heard the long hissing that accompanied the soul leaving the body.

He couldn't rise enough to see if the wolf who'd almost given him Heaven's zip code was moving, but he could make out the mysterious woman laying a palm on Leila's forehead. A bright light shined down from her hand and lit Leila's face. In an instant, her seizing halted, and Anwar knew she was being healed.

The scene lasted seconds, but he could already see Leila was better, as the ashen pallor on her skin began to return to her normal warm brown tone.

As she stepped back and turned to him, he held out a

shaking hand. "No, go to her first. Make sure Farrah is okay," he pleaded. If he had to die, he would go peacefully if it meant his love would be all right.

"She is fine. I would be able to tell if she was dying, but you, on the other hand... You are almost checked out. Let me help you. Then I'll make sure your friend is good."

Anwar wanted to look at Farrah himself, but he found any movement impossible as the tingling sensation swept through his body. "Yeah, fine..." His agreement was reluctant, but without being sure Farrah was out of the woods, he needed to move things along.

"All right. You and the first woman, y'all have been poisoned." She stepped forward and lowered herself to the floor.

"How—how'd you know that?" He barely managed the question as his tongue thickened in his mouth.

"I don't know. I guess I had a vision. Something compelling me to come to this shitty part of town. Now, be still. I'm kind of new to this."

She reached a hand forward; Anwar felt her warm palm touch his forehead before bluish-white light washed him from the inside out. He couldn't explain it, but he felt the closest thing to pure elation in that moment. As her palm heated against his skin, the feeling grew until every part of him felt new.

"All right, that should do it. Now, I'll check the other girl. But then I need to go help... I mean, for some reason, I believe he's my family member, but I don't know how."

He wanted to get up and go to Mael himself, but he wasn't quite right yet.

"She's good. I'll be back. But take them out of here when you can. My vision didn't show me what happens to you. I don't know if there are more wolves... I guess? So, I need you to go."

She offered Anwar a hand, which he accepted. Once he did, she was nearly able to lift him from the ground. Damn, she was strong. And whoever she was, he was glad she'd come along. "Yeah, thanks. I'll get them out of here."

"Okay, I guess I'll see you soon," she said, then she disappeared onto the stairs, moving as if she knew exactly where she was going. And Anwar didn't doubt it.

After a moment of thanking the shit out of the universe, he went to Leila and Farrah, who were both still as disoriented as he was but able to get to their feet. As he made his way out, he looked over at the wolf, half changed back into his human form. His flesh didn't look just broken. His neck appeared to be burned, a black charring that ran from his upper arm all the way to the side of his face.

With a shudder, he moved to get the female he loved to safety. In the back of his mind, he resolved Mael would be okay.

CHAPTER TWENTY-ONE

"Man, I love how you think this is about you. I could have killed you already, but it's almost a joy to afterlife and chill with you. I—"

Goddamn, she was still talking, but at last his hearing fizzled out on him. It was a blessed thing not to hear her droning on and on. "Would you please shut the fuck up," he managed. "That's the problem with narcissists, you know."

The stiletto to the face was probably overkill and had Mael spitting out blood again. Which didn't matter much in the end. She'd poisoned him, and if living meant drinking her rancid-ass blood, he would pass. Especially if there would be no more Lily.

He'd miss his Lily. Regrets flooded through his mind as he let his head loll to the side and the coppery-tasting blood spill from his mouth.

Lily was so goddamned pretty, and she was the only thing that had ever given him a reason to go on. The distant hope that he would see her again. And her smell... fuck, she smelled good.

"Shit, I scuffed my shoe on your ragged-ass teeth. You motherfucker." She kicked him again, this time in the stomach.

With a groan, he let out a hard laugh. "This is getting redundant, isn't it? If you're going to kill me, then fucking do it."

"Yeah, you're right. Then I'll take your head up to Anwar. You see, I ordered them not to kill him. I wanted him to see all of you die before him. You know, I wish I could have shared my plan with my father. He would have been so proud."

"Where's your mother? If she had any common sense, she probably ran far and fast from your jacked-ass family."

"Dead, actually. Yes, my father killed her for sleeping with one of his royal guards. It's okay. I don't miss her. She was always a misfit. Light fae and all."

"Yup, sounds like she got the better end of the deal, for sure."

"All right, that's enough fun. First, I'm going to split those wings you think are so special from your back, then I'll cut your head off. See, I can be merciful too."

She kneeled in, her snarling mug distorting into the true fae features. Her teeth shifted from perfectly even brilliance into dark green spikes, and her brow lifted into arched grooves in her face. Eire and her kind were known for their glamour ability, but only those who were on the verge of death ever saw their true faces. It was one last mind-fuck before they killed their prey. God, they were the worst, Mael thought as he closed his eyes and tried to envision his Lily. She was the one who'd always comforted him, and it was only right that she would be the last thing he thought of as his lights went out for good.

When the sound of meat being cut and a splatter of hot moisture hit his face, he jumped. Eire's scream was loud enough to wake the dead, and the grotesque crunching noise soon blended in with her screams. He wanted to lift himself, but Mael felt disconnected from his body.

In another moment, he felt a hand, then the warmest sensation, like when he was an angel and one of his brothers healed him on the battlefield. Okay, that was not how death should feel. Clearly, he was delusional. Squinting his eyes open in the blinding, blue-tinted glow, he saw only an outline. Could it have been his Lily in her heavenly form? Figured she'd end up an angel, although that wasn't how it usually worked. Humans couldn't be angels, and most vampires—well they wouldn't be allowed in Heaven. Yup, he was losing it.

Maybe that's what death was for his kind. A slow descent into insanity.

Except... he was actually starting to feel better. His mind was able to focus on more than one thing at a time, and his thoughts grew orderly.

"There. You should be good in a second."

But that wasn't... He had heard that voice before, just couldn't place it. Mael attempted to sit upright, but no luck. As good as he felt, the poison was going to take a little while longer to work its way from his system.

"Here," the familiar voice said.

He could feel himself being helped to his feet but couldn't hold his head up to see who it was. Then, after a few steps, he was back on his butt, back to a cold, damp wall. It was then he saw her. Knew who had come to his rescue. What he didn't know was *how*. "Eire..." he asked, his voice still raspy and weak.

"I'm guessing you mean the bitch who was about to kill you? Dead. Now then. Are you my... family member?"

Mael blinked a few times, focusing on her and trying to figure out what to ask first. With so many questions in his mind, he struggled with formulating his thoughts. "Lani... what are you doing here?" It was just as good as any other, he supposed.

"Well, I had a dream like always, but this time, it was more urgent. It always starts like this, I come to find you and you know me... as if for my entire life. The difference was, I still saw things after I opened my eyes. When I woke up, I was still in it with you. Could smell the same funk of the warehouse and spilled blood. It's never happened like this before, at all. So, I followed my instincts, came here, and shot light out of my fucking hands. I mean, how goddamn awesome is that? Oh... Are you an angel? I mean, if you're an angel, I probably shouldn't curse around you, right?"

"Fuck no. I'm not that kind of angel. But"—he groaned as he sought to find at least a little more comfort —"did you happen to see three um... people somewhere on your way down here?" Unsure of how much her dreams had taught her, he erred on the side of caution. Discovering an angel uncle and shooting lights from her hands was probably enough for one night.

"Oh yeah, they're good. I mean, when I left them, they were great."

Mael stared at her for a moment, still kind of unsure whether what was happening was some version of Hell where he would think everything was okay then the rug was snatched from beneath his feet. "This is... this is real, right?"

"I mean, your guess is as good as mine. Normally, I just dream that you watch me while I work. Not just this life, though—like I was in another body... It's kind of weird. My therapist swears it's just a cerebral manifestation of the life I want. A real family, maybe a couple of kids.... Damn. Forgive me for babbling—I just can't believe you're real."

"Yeah, it must be a shock. But, um... there's a female I need to get to. Along the way, I'll tell you some stuff about me, about your father, and about how your life is going to change. It's going to take a long time. Don't worry, though. I swore on your father's deathbed that I would protect you with my dying breath."

"Right, yeah. Like, sure," she said, shaking her head. "I realize this villain's lair is probably not the best place for a reunion, right? And if I may add, that whole protect-me-with-your-dying-breath thing... You probably did that wrong since I'm the one who saved you."

"Yeah..." He chuckled as she hoisted him up from the floor with one hand. "You know, clearly, cynicism runs in the family."

"Now you tell me, after I drove my foster parents nuts over the years."

One thing was for sure, if he was dead, it wasn't as bad as he'd thought it would be.

CHAPTER TWENTY-TWO

FARRAH

Everything hurt. Her legs, her head. There was an acidic taste in her mouth and a burning in the back of her throat. But her senses filled with Anwar. He was near her, somewhere. She squinted her eyes open and found him. He was turned on his side, eyes screwed down tight and brows furrowed. He looked stressed even though he was asleep. She could tell from the even breathing.

Unable to resist, she moved closer to him and softly kissed his lips.

Exactly what she didn't want to happen. Every bone in her body ached with her movement *and* she'd woken him up.

"Farrah..." he whispered, and his features immediately softened.

"Hey, you," she said.

"I thought I'd lost you."

"How'd you find me, anyway?"

"Me, Leila, a little help from Ennis..."

"And Mael, right?"

Anwar didn't reply immediately. His tense jawline worked for a second first. "Yeah, him too."

"Do I want to know what happened between you?" While she couldn't be sure, the tension rolling off Anwar was palpable.

"No. Not right now. I needed to tend to you. I'll deal with him later today. For now, you need your rest, and that is my priority."

"But I have a question," she said, attempting again and failing to scoot closer to him. As if understanding her struggle to get nearer to him, he scooped her body into his. They both moaned a bit at their battered bodies fitting together like pieces of a puzzle. Once settled, Farrah continued. "Do you know why..." She didn't have the energy to finish that question, just trusted he would know.

"Eire was clearly insane. Apparently, there was some plot to get back at me for refusing to marry her. From what we could tell, she was willing to torture you and countless others to get her revenge."

"Oh my God," she said, holding her head up despite the pain. "No one was hurt, were they?"

"Well, yes. All of us were, a bit. But it's okay. Mael's... Well, we don't quite know what she is to him, but we're calling her his niece. She saw our location in a vision. She—"

Before he could finish, all the bloody, graphic memories came back to Farrah in flashes. *Leila...* "Where is Leila?" she blurted.

"She's okay. She is down the hall in what used to be Mael's room."

"What do you mean, *used to be?*"

Anwar stared off for a moment, then heaved a sigh. "It's a long story. It's for the best, for now. At least until we figure out where we are and what happens to Mael's niece. She's a Nephilim. And from what I can tell, she isn't going to be a welcomed presence."

"What the hell happened while I was gone?" Not only was she disoriented from her ordeal, but it seemed the whole world had changed in the blink of an eye.

"Everything... everything happened, but now that I have you back, it's all going to be okay. Speaking of which, you need to feed."

She looked over at him, apprehension filling her. "But aren't you hurt too?"

"I mean... I think *we* should feed."

Everything that had happened in the bathroom when she'd initially brought up the notion of mating flooded her mind. He'd been so leery about it, so concerned... "Anwar, are you sure this is what you want?"

"Have you thought about it?"

"Oh yeah, I mean, even more when I was trapped in that shitty, grave-like basement."

"And would you still have me?"

The words, the beautiful sound of his proposal to mate, were the equivalent of a symphony. She hadn't known she needed to hear them, but they were the salve for her soul. "Yes. I would, Anwar. Forever."

She wanted to make love to him but knew it was probably something her body wouldn't accommodate, so for then, she slowly raised her hand to his lips. In turn, he lifted his to her waiting mouth. As if on some imaginary cue, both bit into one another, and the feeling, the unexpected paradise, filled every part of her. It was better than the sex she still wanted. This was the first time she'd ever known, beyond a shadow of a doubt, she was home.

CHAPTER TWENTY-THREE

eila blinked her eyes open. The first thing she noticed was an aura around her vision, then the blinding pain that shot through her skull.

"Mael, damn you. What are you on the floor for?" She said the words in a whisper, a sign of her exhaustion and so much agony in her chest and head.

"Baby," he growled, the husky tone of sleep in his voice, "you are the balm to my soul right now."

She didn't feel beautiful, nor worthy of the way his eyes lit when he saw her. "I guess. Need help getting off the floor?"

"Nah, I just didn't want you to wake up with a strange angel in your bed."

"Oh yeah. I would have made accommodations for you, though. C'mon up here. You look like shit," she said. Shifting over, she realized she must be in his room at Anwar's. "Damn, how'd I get here?"

"I drove us."

Immediately, panic filled her, overriding even the soreness in her muscles. She was stiff and battered, but he'd better not have wrecked her car. "You can't drive, sir."

In another moment, he was up and on the bed. "Yeah, well, nothing like on-the-job training. Don't worry, I didn't mess up your classic."

To that, she gave him the side-eye.

"Okay. I hit the side of Anwar's garage. But, thankfully, we have a Nephilim in the family. She was able to fix it. As well as the slashed tires."

"The girl," she said, thinking back to the bright light she'd awakened to. After seeing her, she'd passed out almost instantly. But not before witnessing her heal Anwar. "She was... she saved us."

"Yeah. All of us, from a vision she had. I was so... Lily, I was so afraid I'd never see you again. And that I'd never be able to make up for all the pain I've caused you. Not that I think you should take me back. But I just want you to know I'm willing to make it up to you for the rest of your life." Mael looked so sincere, it made her heart ache.

It was too much, though. Too many unanswered questions for her to think of anything else. "Is Farrah—"

"Fine. Everyone is fine."

Though relief flooded her, it was quickly replaced with sadness over all they'd been through together. Her body still ached in places, and the weeks of tension broke inside her. She needed to be held—longed to be comforted. But only by him. "I um... I know I don't have the right, Mael. And you can say no. I'm going to ask anyway." She hesitated, sure she was nudging at an invisible line drawn between them. She'd done some things, taken some liberties with him that stripped her of any rights to his person. To his spirit. Selfish as it was, she pressed forward with her request. "Can you please hold me?"

Mael didn't say anything, just stood and started removing the soiled signature white shirt he wore. Shaking out his wings, he came forth in one fluid movement and slid closer to her on the bed. As she was enveloped in his warmth, the softness of his wings, she curled into him and quietly, without restraint or pretense, openly wept in his arms.

&.

While he wasn't sure how long they'd lain there, holding one another as their aches and pains diminished, Mael only knew it was one of the best times of his life. They were both on the precipice of life-altering events and their futures, hers an ending of her loneliness, his a beginning with whatever he would have to do for Lani, but he didn't care about any of that. If only because he got to comfort Leila in her time of need, everything else, whatever may come, would be all right.

"I'm so sorry," she whispered, hours after she'd shed her first tears. The sun had gone down and come up again before she'd uttered those words.

If he would have had to lie there until the end of time, he would have, but surely, she knew what was in his heart, so he kept that in. "You don't have to be sorry for being vulnerable with me."

"I know, but I've treated you terribly. And after all you've been through. It's... I'm just sorry, that's all. Shit, are you and Anwar okay? He's right down the hall, isn't he?"

"Yes. When we got back here, he told me to take all

the time I need. I will probably have to go somewhere. Do something with Lani, but that can wait. The archangels won't sense her at first. I have a little time to figure out a course of action to keep her safe. So, Anwar and I will work it out. Besides, he has a lot of shit to deal with. I've already spoken with the other members of the Order. Viktoria will be punished for trying to manipulate Anwar into breaking the accords. The Order will want some action. After I told them about my part in the matter, they swore to restrain Viktoria with penalty of death if she ever breathes a word of what happened. And Tarik—well, it was his daughter who did all these things, and he'll have to prove he had no part."

"Do you trust the Order?" she asked, her voice barely more than a whisper.

"I can't say I have a choice. The Order has never been one for being trustworthy. But in this case, they won't want anyone finding out. It could chip away at the already crumbling trust in them to do the right thing."

Lily's hair tickled against his chest as she shook her head. "So, they'll protect your secrets to cover their own asses? It's all too much. I hope everything works out, though."

"Oh, for sure, it'll work out. Besides, Anwar's father awakens soon. Atlanteans have to rest after a thousand years. Constantine's been asleep for a while, and soon, the Order will have to deal with his wrath."

"I never liked the Order, nor what they stand for. They're just a bunch of fucking politicians."

"Yeah, well, let's not spend all our time talking about them. I don't know how long you'll let me lie here without trying to kill me. And before you ask, I took all the glass out of the room."

The smack against his chest rang out in the space. "Don't give me ideas."

"See, there it is. I knew you were just waiting for the right time."

She pulled away and laughed, her gorgeous lips spread over her soul-piercing smile. "My God, do you ever stop being sarcastic?"

"No. Never. But if you want me to stop, I will. I'd do anything for you, Lily." Fuck, he hadn't meant to say it. With it in the air, though, he was glad he'd done it. She needed to know. Needed to understand how his world stopped existing when he'd thought she was no longer in it.

Abruptly, her giggles stopped, and she stilled in his arms. "Mael, I c—"

"I know, Lily. I know you can't be with me again. And I understand what I did. I just wanted you to know, to get that the only reason I was ever able to go on was because I knew you were somewhere living your very best life. Even if you weren't with me, I could lie down at night knowing you were somewhere under the same sky. That's it."

"Has anyone ever told you that you talk too much?"

"I can honestly say everyone I've ever met has told me to shut up at least once."

"And you can't take a hint, huh? I was going to say I could stay here with you forever. Yes, there is uncertainty, and I will have to deal with my own grief first, but I was ready to take you back nearly the moment you stepped into Melody that day. That's why I was so angry with you. I thought if I pushed hard enough, you would leave." Leila sat up and stared at him before placing a hand on his cheek and tracing the outline of his jaw. "And I could go back to my sad little life. In the years we were apart, I learned a valuable skill—faking it. I was the life of the party, the strong one, the star performer in a one-female act. And I was miserable beneath it all. Yes, you left. But it was due to loyalty. Still, pain had become my friend, and I wasn't ready to let her go. Not just yet."

Overwhelming. That's how her truth stirred inside him. It was impossible to believe she could give him another chance after he'd done so much wrong. And even more, the possibility that she could love him again over-shadowed all the troubles he still faced. "Please, Lily... please don't say these things if you don't mean them. I wouldn't be able to take it."

"No, I mean it. I was just so caught up in the dangers of letting my guard down again that I couldn't see how much you'd changed. Sure, you're still impossible to deal with and talk about sixty percent more than you listen, but those were some of the things I adored about you. You've always been my polar opposite. And that's what makes you... well, one of my favorite males."

"Lily, I swear on my life, on my wings, that I will not ever hurt you again. You know that, right? I mean, you understand that I am yours forever, no matter what may come?"

"See, it's that kind of shit that I don't stand a chance against." Biting into her lower lip, she smiled at him.

Unable to resist her another second, he grabbed her neck and pulled her mouth close to his own. "I need to kiss you, but if you tell me you don't want this right now, I won't. I just need to hear you say you want me too." His voice carried all the things he didn't want her to see—his fear of rejection by her, his desperation to be with her, and his inability to control his actions. He dropped the bravado and allowed her to see inside him.

"No... no, Mael, I don't want you. I need you."

As if a spear hit him through the heart, he was stunned still, his body stiffening along with his cock as every part of him surrendered to her. "Dammit, Lily..." In a rush, he captured her mouth with his own and fell into her, his body wildly, yet carefully, folding over hers as they lay back on the bed.

Their kiss was a savage exploration of one another. Her hands were on his wings, the featherlight stroke just right to bring him to a fever pitch. He wanted to touch her everywhere, angry that his hands could only cover so much skin at a time. He caressed her, from breast to ass and back again as he indulged in her.

He hated to back off as she pulled at her shirt and slipped her pants off her long, toned legs. Lily was, and had always been, everything he desired in a female. Despite their differences, she had filled all the broken spaces with her love, her devotion to him. It was that exact quality that made her so special to him.

When she was naked, he had to take her all in. Allowing his eyes to rove over her silky skin, he could only think of how she was way too good for him. As greedy and selfish as he was, he was unable to leave her alone, though. He wanted her so desperately.

Lowering his head, he suckled her breast while running a single finger down her belly to dip inside the place that may as well have been his true north. Her sex, wet and anxious for him, nearly brought him to orgasm from a single touch. He shuddered as she arched her body and moaned out his name.

"Mael..." she whispered, the teasing in her sensual tone serving only to make his ministrations over her body more desperate.

When he couldn't stand it anymore, he stripped his pants off, probably tearing them at the seams.

He was back on her so fast, he prayed she hadn't missed him. Taking one leg, he anchored it over his shoulder and surged upward, pressing his cock against her pussy. He wanted to play a bit before he allowed himself the unadulterated ecstasy of entering her. "Tell me you want me," he demanded, right before placing one long lick up her neck.

"Damn you, Mael, I want you. Please…"

"That's it. You do remember." He laughed against her throat. "And if I don't?"

"You are gonna fuck around and find out. Now, give it to me," she cried out, the lilt of her voice light and carefree, tinted with pleading.

Unable to stand the wait anymore himself, he pressed his erection into her waiting slit. It was pure Heaven on Earth, as if her body was made to fit him perfectly. As he entered her, Lily dragged her nails down his back before bringing her hands back up to stroke the delicate flesh beneath his wings.

Mael knew what he was missing, and it was something he'd dreamed of for a lifetime. Pressing his neck to her lips, he slid his hand under her neck. "Feed from me, Lily." Mael had always taken a perverse pleasure in her taking his blood. It was everything to serve her in such a way, and while it was and would forever be his favorite fantasy to come to life, the real thing made him speed up as he moved inside her.

"You are a bad boy, Mael," she scolded.

It was the last thing he registered before the pinch of her fangs, then the erotic drags she took of his blood stripped away his senses. He couldn't breathe nor control himself as he drove into her at an ever-quickening pace. When he could take no more, every part of him stiffened, and his wings concaved around them as if to keep them tethered together through the torrents of their lovemaking.

He could feel her tighten around him. Just as he had a preoccupation with her fangs, she was completely indulgent when it came to his wings. Deviously, he used the tips of his feathers to caress her skin, and as he expected, she came apart in his arms. With a curse on her lips, she cried out for him, begging him not to stop. Her body arched and stiffened beneath him as she spoke in the language of desire, soft gasps and moans on her full lips.

It was then, only when he had brought her all the pleasure his angelic body had to give, that he allowed himself to release. Inside her, this was his Heaven. Leaving it behind had been his Hell. And as long as he lived, there would never, ever be another place for him save by her side.

When they came to a rest, both of them sated, spent, and wrapped in one another's arms, he knew he had to reveal the one thing he had never told her. With a slight shift, he pulled her on top of him and held her close.

"Lily..."

"Hmm," she said, her voice languid to match her body.

"I knew the first day I met you that you were my forever."

She trembled in his arms again, then smiled up at him. "Then don't leave me again."

Sliding his hand down her back, he cupped her ass in his palm. "Fortunately, I'm well past my stupid stage. I just hope you don't wake up and realize I don't deserve you."

"Oh baby, don't worry. I realized that some time ago."

"I think that deserves a little punishment, doesn't it?" With one roll, he was back on top of her, sliding inside her and making up for all the time they'd lost.

"Wait... I've got something to tell you."

Reluctantly, he slowed his stroke and tried to focus through the blur his mind became when he made love to her. "What is it?" he asked.

"I still have the necklace, Mael. I just didn't want to tell you then. But... I couldn't bear to get rid of it. I... I hope you aren't angry with me," she said, wrapping her arms around his neck.

"No, I'm not mad. And while that tore me apart in the moment, I meant what I said. I shouldn't have done that to you. And you don't have to worry about me ever putting you in that position again. I will protect you, Lily. Forever and always."

Mael knew, of course, that forever would never be enough of his love. He would, however, enjoy every single minute of his Lily for as long as they had together.

CHAPTER TWENTY-FOUR

Mael had lost track of the days that had passed since he'd last walked into the Westborn Penthouse belonging to Anwar and Constantine. Things had been resolved with the Order—Viktoria having been removed due to her malfeasance and treachery, and Constantine would be installed as its leader upon his awakening. Mael had even convinced Tarik to aid in his efforts to cloak Lelania from the archangels, at least until he could figure out a plan. With her powers on full display, he would need all the assistance he could get with keeping her hidden. It was one thing to hide her as a human, but a signature was left each time powers were used. Her signature would be different from Mael's and, therefore, traceable. Hopefully, he'd come up with a plan before the end of her fifty years, if that even mattered anymore. That was something only time would tell.

There was one thing left: mending the divide between him and Anwar. And though it would have been tempting to just leave things as they were, Mael had learned his lesson on simply walking away from those he cared about.

He knew Farrah was at VMA, so there was no better time for them to air out their grievances. Well, Anwar would probably be the one doing all the venting. And Mael had resolved to just let him talk.

The door opened, and the familiar, big body filled the space. Anwar, despite what Mael had expected, didn't immediately punch him in the face. "Mael..." he said. His voice was practically a snarl, but still... better than nothing.

"Hey. I thought we should do this face to face, brother."

Without a word of acknowledgment, Anwar turned, walked back into the expansive room, and took a seat. There was a glass of whiskey on the end table next to him, and as soon as he was in his seat, he lifted it and downed the entire contents. "I was wondering how long it would take for you to find your way back here."

Mael stepped over to the window and stared out over the Detroit River. The body of water was never truly still. It was always choppy, the currents stirring beneath, even on a cold, windless November night. "I've been thinking on it for a while. Thought you would need time to sort out your feelings."

"Or you needed time to sort out yours. Kind of cowardly, don't you think?"

Mael bristled but didn't turn to face his old friend. Didn't debate the validity of the statement. Anwar was right, after all. "I didn't want to have this conversation. Not just yet. And yeah, since you bring it up, I was afraid. I had been for a long time. Viktoria had me in a bad spot, but I won't blame her. This was me. I should have come to you. I was a coward. I didn't own up to my actions with Azazel, nor with Leila. And certainly not with you."

This silence that followed was enough to make Mael turn around to confront the closest male to him since he'd fallen. Anwar sat in his chair, the brown leather broken in around him after so many years. He'd dragged it with him no matter where he and Constantine had lived.

With a slow pace to the couch opposite Anwar, Mael took his chosen place. How many nights had they sat in those exact spots, shooting the shit? The memories flooded in, reminding him of all he'd miss if Anwar decided not to forgive him, as was his right. "I apologize. My actions could have ruined you and your family. And for that, I will never be able to forgive myself."

"I thought of what I would say when I saw you again. It was inevitable, you know? As close as Leila and Farrah are, we were bound to cross paths again. To be perfectly frank, it's hard to watch my Farrah suffer through this. Your relationship with Leila makes it difficult for them to spend time together, and they are effectively bearing the brunt of your betrayal." Cold, dark eyes lit from within, the anger illuminating them in golden brilliance. They would have been beautiful if not so horrifying.

"I have noticed, as well. Leila wants Farrah at her side. But I am a barrier. And I am willing to do anything—save leaving her. I made a vow that I would never do that again." This he meant with all his heart and soul. As much as he cared for Anwar, there was nothing that would compare to his love and devotion to Leila. Not anything or anyone could hold a candle to what he felt for her.

"It didn't have to come to this, Mael. You could have told me what she was doing. The things you did wouldn't have made me look at you as less than my brother. You were my confidant and kinsman. Did you not realize that?"

The knot in Mael's gut tensed, a relentless vise that choked the words from his throat. He could not say anything in the moment. Instead, he simply nodded. Listening, instead of talking, for a change.

"It will take me a while to forget what happened... In fact, I don't know if I ever will, given what was at stake."

Finding his words, Mael cleared his throat. "I understand. In fact, I expected—"

"But I forgive you."

Surely, Mael had heard him incorrectly. "You what?"

"I said I forgive you. While it's hard to understand, I can't say I wouldn't have done the same thing. Farrah shared with me who Lani is and how she came to be. In fact, Tarik imparted how strong she is. The reason she is so feared by the angels. I get that the secrecy of her existence has depended on you."

"So, I sent him a message asking for his strict confidence regarding his knowledge of who she is We can't have any other species knowing about her. I don't know if they're ready. And there's no way to know what will happen to her in the future."

"As you should have. But I don't think we'll have to worry about him. The Order has agreed to suppress his daughter's actions to save him ridicule and shame among the fae. As vain as they are, they would never stand for a king who had such scandal in his family."

Mael nodded. "I'm surprised at the Order for being so cooperative."

"They didn't have a choice, really. Viktoria left them in a precarious situation. They have to act." Anwar swirled his drink again, staring into the glass before continuing. "So, you wanna tell me about all this?" Anwar stood from his seat and walked back to the bar.

"From the top?" Mael asked. Despite his reluctance, he owed Anwar that much.

If they were ever to rebuild their friendship, it would have to be from a place of honesty. And respect.

Something Mael would never take for granted again. Not when it came to the people he loved.

THE END

ACKNOWLEDGMENTS

This series is probably the one that I held closest to my heart for so long. Even when I wanted to turn my back on the whole thing, Sara Megibow, my agent never let me forget how much I loved the story. I so appreciate your support. To my friends and family, as always, your love and encouragement serves as the wind beneath my wings.

To my besties – Amalie, MK, Sage, Shaila, and Sienna - y'all are so incredibly awesome and I don't think I would have made this writing thing work without our DMs and Girl's nights.

Thanks to my editor, Jennifer, for not allowing me to miss a beat! Rockstar status!

To all those readers, fans, and my Street Team – the Angels, I do this for you and pour a little of my soul into every word. Thank you for your continued support. I can't tell you how much I appreciate being on your e-reader/audio/bookshelf.

And to everyone I mentioned and all those I may have forgotten, remember that love is the most important thing. And I do love each of you.

Always Shine Bright
Aliza M

AUTHOR BIO

Aliza has only ever wanted to write. Throughout her professional career in healthcare, raising two children, and eating her weight in chocolate, she never deviated from her dreams of one day, adding the notch of novelist to her belt. Author of paranormal and contemporary novels with their strong, quirky heroines in common, she continues to write the love stories of her heart. And perhaps, still eats just a little too much chocolate. For more by Aliza Mann, visit her website at www.alizamannauthor.com.